LEGACY

H.M. BAILEY

LEGACY

This is a work of fiction. All of the characters, names, incidents, organizations, and dialogue in this novel are either the products of the author's imagination or are used fictitiously.

iUniverse books may be ordered through booksellers or by contacting:

iUniverse
1663 Liberty Drive
Bloomington, IN 47403
www.iuniverse.com
1-800-Authors (1-800-288-4677)

Because of the dynamic nature of the Internet, any web addresses or links contained in this book may have changed since publication and may no longer be valid. The views expressed in this work are solely those of the author and do not necessarily reflect the views of the publisher, and the publisher hereby disclaims any responsibility for them.

Any people depicted in stock imagery provided by Getty Images are models, and such images are being used for illustrative purposes only.
Certain stock imagery © Getty Images.

ISBN: 978-1-5320-9025-7 (sc)
ISBN: 978-1-5320-9024-0 (e)

Library of Congress Control Number: 2019920200

Print information available on the last page.

iUniverse rev. date: 03/04/2021

Sometimes the people around you won't understand your journey. They don't need to, it's not for them."

— Joubert Botha

PROLOGUE

The bullet-riddled panel van, ironically painted gunmetal grey, came to a grinding halt as black smoke billowed from the smashed hood. The two driver's side tires were flat, causing the old panel van to drift into the only lamp post located in the deserted cul de sac. Darkness overtook the uninhabited, partially constructed neighborhood. In the distance, four approaching xenon headlights infiltrated the blackness as they drew close. Two silver supercharged Range Rovers came to a screeching halt approximately 20 yards from the commandeered work van.

From each of the high line vehicles stepped three men. Adorned on each of the men was a fitted dark blue pinstriped suit with black silk shirts buttoned to the neck. Their shiny black alligator skin shoes and their custom designer black sunglasses reflected the moonlight. The men made their way towards the van with such grace, similar to models on a Milan runway. Each of the men had earpieces that allowed them to communicate with the last occupant left in the Range Rover, but no one spoke. The men gave quick hand signals as they quickly flanked the van, surrounding it on all four sides. From underneath their suit jackets, each of the men unholstered their modified semi-automatic weapon. The guns were no doubt the reason for the porous van that stood before them. The men all looked at each other and nodded as they approached, their weapons trained on the van.

A large mahogany-skinned man with massive dreadlocks studied the six approaching men from the van's driver's seat.

"They're trying to flank us," the petite blonde woman queried from the rear of the van as she leaned her head against the van's side door and peered through one of the countless bullet holes.

It was a miracle; neither she nor Enali, the handsome gentleman behind the steering wheel, had not been struck by the armor-piercing divine bullets. The woman's silent prayer of appreciation was interrupted by the small gurgle coming from the three-month-old resting on the floor of the cargo van wrapped in dirty painter's sheets.

"Shhhh, it's okay, my sweet boy," the woman said, reassuringly looking away from the approaching mercenaries. "We should just ask for forgiveness and accept our punishment."

"Forgiveness is for those who have done something wrong. All we've done is love each other, Illyana," Enali spoke as he too took his eyes off of the approaching men and looked in the rearview mirror at the mother of his child. Looking at Illyana instantly replaced the rage that boiled in Enali. The feeling was hard for a demon like him to explain. It was like summer lighting was running through his veins every time he gazed at Illyana, who was the most beautiful person he had ever known. Her physical beauty was breathtaking, but her kindness and ability to see the good in everyone, even him, was what captivated his dark heart. As Enali searched for words to comfort his love, he could find none, so he just smiled. Illyana smiled back and blushed. They had taken a risk. They had broken the rules, but it had been worth it. Illyana looked down at her son and knelt, placing a kiss on his forehead.

"Enali, you know we will have to kill them for him to live."

"Every last one," Enali said sinisterly as a black mist began to cover his body. The fog swirled around his six-foot-four athletic frame and densified into impenetrable black armor covering him from head to toe. "I'll take the one directly in front of the van and the two on the passenger side. I'll draw them off, and you and the boy make your way to their car and drive off. I'll meet you once it's all over," Enali said, his deep voice echoing through the armor that encased his face.

"No, my love. There's no way you can take on an archangel and his security detail. You know he's around, creepily waiting in the shadows. You will die if I do not help," Illyana said as she pulled her dirty blond hair into a ponytail. From under her tattered dress, she pulled two pearl-handled karambits and slid her fingers into the rings, and clenched her fists. "I'll take the one in front of the van and the two on the passenger side. You clear the rest, and then we both make a break for the car closest to the street. Be fast, and make your strikes count. These men are here for our son, and they will stop at nothing until he's dead."

The six men approaching the van stopped in their tracks. Muffled voices were coming from the van. Each man turned on the light attachments on their weapons, but the light reflected onto their designer shades. The dark smog that covered Enali had now taken a liquid form and had begun overflowing from the wrecked van. Each of the six men took a few steps back, not wanting the demonic toxin to touch them while keeping their eyes trained on the van.

From the murky darkness that once resembled a windshield, Illyana launched herself at the man closest to the hood of the wrecked van, her karambits slicing the man's throat as she thudded into him. The pinstriped suit assassin instantly grasped at his throat, allowing Illyana to plunge her karambits into each side of the man's torso. With one fluent motion, Illyana cut up and through, disemboweling the assassin on the deserted street. The two men on the passenger side of the van trained their weapons to fire, but Illyana had already disarmed and cleared the disemboweled man's weapon and was already in motion. Illyana rolled as the two men fired, their bullets striking their fallen counterpart. Illyana steadied herself and fired two shots. The divine light bullets whistled through the night air, hitting the assailants in their heads, dropping them instantly.

The two men who flanked the driver's side of the vehicle and the one from the rear of the van tried to come to the aid of their fallen brothers, but their path was obscured by a six-foot-four mass of darkness that had appeared out of nowhere. The men raised their weapons, but in the dark, Enali was in his element. Enali teleported into the night, reappearing in an instant and then vanishing. The razor-sharp talons of the demonic armor sliced through the guns and their wielders like paper. Like a feral cat, Enali toyed with his attackers merely for his entertainment, dragging out their suffering before their inevitable conclusion. With his bare hands, Enali smashed the men's heads against the van. Their once black suits were now maroon tinged in the moonlight. Illyana looked at Enali and rolled her eyes lovingly. Enali shrugged and smile, the armor evaporating from his face.

"You said to make it quick; our definition of quick is just different," Enali said as he opened the van door to grab his son. A phosphorus-lit white-bladed sword pierced him through his armor and straight into his heart in a blinding flash of light.

"Enali!" Illyana screamed as she raced towards the van. Enali looked at the man who had stabbed him and shook his head in disbelief. Standing in the van next to his son was an aged, tall, slender, well-dressed man with pale white skin and even paler hair. The man's ice-blue eyes stared at Enali with hate and admiration. The man put his wing-tipped alligator skinned shoe on Enali's chest and kicked the armored demon while pulling the sword from his body. The blade made a sloshing noise as it reversed its course from Enali's torso.

Illyana caught and guided Enali as he stumbled and fell to the ground. Enali looked down at the hole in his chest and struggled to speak as blood pooled in his mouth.

"Protect my son," Enali sputtered.

Defiantly Illyana pulled her karambits and prepared to face the attacker.

"Come on now. You know you can't beat me, child," the man said condescendingly from the van placing the flaming sword on the floor. The blade sizzled, still fresh with Enali's blood leaving an aroma of burning flesh.

Illyana screamed as she dived into the van. Aware of her son on the floor, Illyana quickly attempted to close the space between her and her attacker. Her karambits were close contact weapons, and she planned on putting them to use as she tried to protect her son. Though her attacks were precise, the slender man laughed as he playfully dodged all of her attacks with ease. During the brief encounter, the man was able to disarm Illyana of her karambit's and slice through the tendons above both knees so she couldn't stand. Dragging herself along the floor of the van Illyana tried to grab the man who was now standing over her son. The man kicked the crawling mother in the face.

"Look what you made me do!" The man exclaimed fitfully. "You have always been a defiant one, my beautiful Illyana."

Illyana watched helplessly as the man knelt, picked up his discarded sword, and made his way towards her son. The baby looked up from the floor of the van at the man who stood above him and began to coo.

"He's not afraid of you," Illyana said, laughing.

"Then, like his mother, he is a fool," the slender man said apologetically, raising his sword, which had begun to burn brighter.

"No, he's his father's son," Illyana responded, looking at the dead body of Enali vacant of all of his dark armor.

The lean man's eyes grew wide, realizing that the demonic armor had vacated Enali's lifeless body and quickly brought his sword down on the baby. The blade shattered, sending flaming metallic shrapnel throughout the van. Enali's impenetrable armor now covered the baby. The armor of legend molded in the deepest depths of hell could learn to adapt to attacks and couldn't be harmed by the same violation twice. As the pale assassin continued to try and strike the baby, Illyana began to laugh.

"In the end, Enali finally beat you. We beat you. Our love beat you."

The assassin stood up in the van, slicked his white hair back, composed himself, and picked up part of his shattered blade. He smiled remorsefully as he made his way over to Illyana and leaned down. The assassin lovingly moved Illyana's hair from her face and spoke to her tenderly.

"Dear child, we could've had it all. Make no mistake, but your death will haunt me forever, but you brought this on yourself."

The assassin plunged the shattered blade into Illyana's chest. Illyana gasped and looked lovingly at her son resting on the floor, his body encased in armor, and smiled. After watching the life leave his former students' eyes, the assassin remorsefully stood up and exited the vehicle. He gathered his slaughtered six security detail members, along with Enali's limp body, and tossed them in the van with ease. Grabbing a full gas can from one of the Range Rovers, the well-dressed assassin doused the corpse-filled van and the remaining Range Rovers in gasoline. The killer struck a match and threw it into the van. The van erupted in flames and quickly spread to the armored Range Rovers.

"Fire, the ultimate cleanser of life," the slender assassin said as he disappeared into the night.

Surrounded by death and destruction, the child cried out to the darkness, but his cries went unanswered in the night.

To different minds, the same world is a hell,
and heaven - Ralph Waldo Emerson

CHAPTER

An old faded Red Pony Cafe digital clock hung over the dimly lit bar. The clock struggled to cut through the dense cigarette smoke as it ticked down to the New Year. Old and new friends were all preparing to say goodbye to last year with all its disappointments, missed goals, setbacks, and hello to the New Year, with all its unlimited potential. New Year a New You weight loss pamphlets littered the floor of the small bar. The neighborhood weight watchers group was looking to recruit new clients and had dropped off several packs of booklets. The pamphlets that hadn't made it to the floor were now being used as coasters and handheld fans. The bars exhaust fans were trying extremely hard to evacuate the thick cigarette smoke but were not up to the task due to their age and lack of required maintenance. The four outdated analog televisions positioned around the small bar simultaneously broadcasted the famous New Years' ball countdown in Times Square.

"Three, two, one. Happy New Year!" The cramped crowd of approximately 40 people, with staff included, erupted in cheer.

Kurt Bryant watched from his position at the back sink that was overflowing with dishes as everyone hugged each other and wished each other a Happy New Year. Kurt looked away from the crowd and back at the massive pile of dishes awaiting him and closed his eyes. Breathing deeply, Kurt tried to get the approaching anxiety under control. Today was January first, which meant it was New Year's Day, but it also meant today was his birthday.

Kurt had never cared about his birthday as a child, and as an adult, he still harbored the same feelings. Kurt had a morbid yet unique outlook regarding birthdays, especially his own. Every year he aged, he was one step closer to the end of his life. Kurt had never understood the anticipation of birthdays. Each year on the same day, people got excited to celebrate what exactly. If you were fortunate, people gave you gifts in honor of your day of birth that you had absolutely no control over. Kurt felt that if people genuinely cared about someone, why didn't they give you a gift every day? Just a phone call saying hey, just thinking about you, or just wanting to say that if you need anything, I'm here. Instead, birthday cards arrived in the mail from relatives wishing you a happy birthday. Sometimes these cards would contain cash, gift cards, or lottery tickets. Lifelong friends took you out to lunch or threw you a surprise party, only to forget you for the next three hundred and sixty-four days. Conceivably life had tainted Kurt's birthday views. Kurt had never received a birthday gift or a card from a distant relative or anyone in all of his twenty-one years of existence. Growing up in the Washington D. C. foster care system had fashioned Kurt's distinctive views regarding birthdays. Birthdays spent with loved ones was probably exciting, but Kurt had been a number and a monthly stipend in an endless system of despair and futility.

No foster family ever wanted to keep Kurt for long due to his exclusive personality. He was a burdensome, stressed, anxiety-riddled child, and odd occurrences seemed to follow him from home to home. The sullen child that was Kurt Bryant was something of a perplexity. Mix the oddities and the x-file like occurrences that followed him, and it wasn't hard to see why Kurt was transferred continuously to different foster homes on such a regular basis. Kurt's juvenile case file was so thick that it took up an entire file cabinet in the department of social services. Kurt Bryant was the first pre-teen to have his file marked as unplaceable. While most toddlers could be placed with ease, Kurt managed to get returned every time. When Kurt was four years old and in his seventh foster home, several of the older irksome adolescent foster children pushed Kurt down a flight of stairs because they thought it would be entertaining. When Kurt hit the bottom of the stairs, he did not cry like most toddlers. Instead, Kurt stood up, glared, and pointed at his attackers, who were standing at the top of the stairs when the entire stairwell spontaneously erupted into flames, severely burning one of the minors. As Kurt grew older, he developed other peculiar tendencies that did not help him to make friends. By the time he was ten, and in his twenty-third foster home, Kurt had taken to sitting alone in the dark for hours on end. While in the darkness, Kurt would carry on conversations with himself. To the adults, it looked as if Kurt was talking to an imaginary friend. However, all the voices inside his head were, in fact, authentic. Several therapists agreed that it was a cry for attention from a child who just wanted to feel loved.

At the age of fifteen, the state placed Kurt in his forty-ninth foster home. This foster home was run by one of the pillars in the foster care community named Gladys Morris. Some of her foster children that she had adopted had become doctors, lawyers, and even city councilwomen. Gladys Morris had a reputation for molding the worst children into some of the best children through hard work and strict rules. Who would ever think anything horrible about a sixty-three-year-old God-fearing white grandmother? The Sunday school teacher demeanor also helped. There had been rumors of abuse, but it was overlooked due to Gladys's track record. No sooner had Kurt's overworked and underpaid social worker pulled away in her state-appointed teal van when the emotional abuse began. Gladys looked at Kurt over her coke bottle glasses and told him she would fuck him up in ways he couldn't imagine if he messed with her money. Raising foster kids was her job, and some crazy high yellow nut job wasn't going to ruin a good thing. Gladys explained to Kurt that she had ways of making people disappear since one of her biological adult children Leroy, Bubba for short, worked on a fishing boat in Louisiana. Human flesh was said to be a sufficient bait when trying to catch alligators. Gladys showed Kurt to his room, a small utility closet that housed a broken water heater and an outdated electrical panel box. Kurt was allowed out of his room to eat, shower, use the bathroom, go to school, and talk to his social worker when she dropped by for her scheduled visits.

Unlike the other foster children who lived in the house and had to endure similar living conditions, Kurt never once cried out or complained; he appreciated the time to himself. In the lightless room, he was free to be himself and converse with the voices that inhabited his mind. Like all of the brief moments of happiness in Kurt's life, this, too, was short-lived. One night after Gladys had come home from bingo in one of her losing moods, she banished Kurt and the other foster children to their makeshift rooms without dinner. When one of the younger children, a nine-year-old girl who hadn't been in Gladys's care for long, began to protest, Gladys angrily struck the child. Gladys would've hit the young girl again if Kurt hadn't intervened by stepping between the old caretaker and the crying child.

"Don't touch her again, Ms. Gladys," Kurt whispered.

"Or what you bat shit crazy asshole!" Gladys spat angrily in Kurt's face, her breath smelling of cheap peppermint liquor. "If I do hit this ungrateful little bitch what are you going to do about it?"

Nothing ma'am, Kurt thought. "We will end your miserable existence, you diabetic drunk cow," Kurt said, surprised at the outburst. The voices in his head had hijacked his mouth and continued to speak. "We could leave you to your own devices since you're one potted meat sandwich away from a heart attack anyway."

Gladys looked at Kurt in astonishment and started to laugh. "I was your last stop, and you just blew it by threatening me. No one wanted to foster an old weirdo, but I allowed you in my home. Do you think I need the measly twelve hundred dollars I get a month for you? All the bureaucratic bullshit I went through for you. I practically had to beg your social worker not to send you to one of those boys' homes. Well, I'm going to show you what happens to unappreciative little shits like you. First thing tomorrow, I'm calling your social worker and having you yanked out of here. I hope she was worth it," Gladys said, referring to the young child Kurt spoke up to protect. "Have a good night's sleep because it's the last one you'll have here," Gladys called out as she drunkenly made her way upstairs to her room.

Mrs. Gladys, I'm sorry! Please don't send me away, Kurt thought, but again his mouth betrayed him. "No, sweetheart, it is you who will be having their last sleep here," Kurt called out after Gladys.

Around two a. m Kurt awoke to intense black smoke coming from the old, outdated electrical panel. The copper pipes from the top of the panel that ran up the wall were flaming red hot. Thinking quickly, Kurt ran from the closet and began calling out to everyone in the house."

Fire! Fire! Everyone get out!" Kurt screamed at the top of his lungs as he went from room to room.

As Kurt bounded the stairs for Gladys's room, he suddenly stopped in his tracks. A large black wolf with crimson eyes emerged from Gladys's room and blocked Kurt's path through the smoke. The wolf's fur was blacker than black, as if it was part of the dark shadows that covered the hallway. The wolf made sure to stay out of the light of the fire to remain camouflaged in the darkness. The wolf's red eyes were focused on Kurt, studying him, measuring him up for an attack. Hair and chunks of flesh hung from the mouth of the creature. Kurt slowly tried to get around the wolf to enter Gladys's room, but the wolf mirrored Kurt's movements blocking his path. The wolf looked at Kurt and howled. Kurt covered his ears and looked away in fear. The howling stopped, and when Kurt looked, the spot that the wolf occupied some moments ago was vacant.

Incredibly that night, not one foster child was hurt, but the fire claimed Gladys Morris's life. Authorities traced the fire's origin to the faulty, outdated circuit panel in Kurt's makeshift bedroom. Upon further investigation, facts came to light regarding how badly the foster children were physically and emotionally abused while in Gladys's care. Not wanting to discredit a pillar in the foster care community, the state didn't complete a thorough investigation. The state, not wanting a scandal, quickly relocated all of the foster children except Kurt. It didn't help that Kurt told anyone who would listen about the wolf that came out of Gladys's room the night her house burned down. Fearing that Kurt would find someone to listen to his absurd story and cause someone to look deeper into Gladys and her abuse, Kurt was sent to an all-boys military school for eighteen months until the chaos died down. While in the military school, Kurt was prescribed pills to help calm his vivid imagination. Not wanting to be medicated, Kurt pretended to swallow his medications, but he was wisely hiding them under his tongue until he could flush them. Quickly realizing that he was different and being different was terrible, Kurt pretended to be ordinary. When the voices in his head spoke, Kurt would ignore them until he was alone or knew that no one was watching. Kurt was tired of being discarded like weekly trash, so he decided he would do whatever he had to do to fit in.

Kurt made up his mind that he would have to take care of himself because no one else would ever care for him. Kurt finished his year and a half in military school and was placed back into the foster care system. Within a few months of searching for a new foster home, it was determined that Kurt would live out his years in a group home until he aged out at eighteen. No one wanted to foster an awkward, introverted teenager whose file was full of unexplainable issues. One week shy of his eighteenth birthday, Kurt skipped school due to the unrelenting chatter from the voices in his head and decided to take a stroll into the working district of Washington D. C. to apply for jobs. Since he had no particular skills, Kurt elected to be a typical teenager by applying to several local restaurants. Kurt was willing to do anything as long as it kept him away from the group home where he lived and the voices in his head somewhat occupied.

The last restaurant that Kurt applied to was a newly opened Jamaican restaurant called Dawns. Evelynn Thomas, a former Jamaican model and a sixth-generation bar owner interviewed Kurt and hired him on the spot to sweep floors and do dishes. Evelynn felt somewhat obligated to give Kurt a job. She knew this town and knew that none of the other restaurants would give a young African American man a chance. Washington D. C., home of the most powerful government globally, had a racial discrimination problem that no one addressed. Young men like Kurt ended up in jail, or worse, murdered by the police who swore to protect them. Evelynn told Kurt that the pay wasn't great and that there would be no chance of a pay raise any time soon. To Evelynn's surprise, the gawky, reclusive teenager in front of her said he just wanted to fill his time after school so he wouldn't have to spend the afternoons in the group home where he lived. There was something that drew Evelynn to Kurt. Evelynn could see that Kurt had been knocked down, yet the young man kept on with his head up and continued to carry on.

If anyone knew about hard times, it was Evelynn Thomas. Evelynn had recently lost her wife Dawn to breast cancer three months prior after a seven-year battle, and now she was a single mother of two. Everyday Evelynn had to will herself to go on, and she felt Kurt had to do the same. Every day after school and even on the weekends, Kurt would show up at Dawns to work. Evelynn had never seen anyone so happy to sweep up dirt in her entire life. There were times when Evelynn swore she would see Kurt talking to himself while he was working, but whenever Kurt would notice her looking, he would smile awkwardly and wave. Evelynn admired Kurt's dedication and meticulous ways of doing things. Whatever tasks Evelynn would give Kurt, he would get them done efficiently and correctly. Before long, Evelynn, the beautiful Jamaican bar owner with chestnut skin and a perfect smile, took Kurt under her wing and began mentoring the young boy. Unlike his times in foster care, Kurt believed that Evelynn cared for him.

After a few months of working at Dawns, Evelynn introduced Kurt to her two children Jacob and Leah. In no time, Kurt became friends with Evelynn's seventeen-year-old son Jacob. After his mother died, Jacob had become quiet and withdrawn from the world. Somehow Kurt bought Jacob out of his shell. Around Kurt, Jacob didn't have to pretend that everything was okay. Kurt knew Jacob was sad and didn't pressure Jacob to talk about his feelings. When Jacob was ready to open up, Kurt would be there to listen. Most days, the two boys would watch what Jacob called Black Exploitation movies or listen to classic Jamaican records. Kurt loved how both the songs and films told stories about overcoming and never giving up. When the two boys weren't listening to music or reciting lines from the movies they had watched hundreds of times, they would talk about their futures. Jacob was an athlete who said he would be the next Usain Bolt. Kurt would laugh as Jacob would describe how he'd race into the history books as the fastest man alive. Kurt would change the subject when it was his turn to talk about his future. Kurt didn't want to worry about what the future held because Kurt was content with living in the present for the first time in his life.

If Evelynn Thomas had any idea that Kurt had a massive crush on her daughter Leah, she never let on that she knew. Leah's temperament was similar to Kurt's. She, too, was uncharacteristic. While most sixteen-year-old girls were concerned about going to the mall and partying, Leah was not. Leah also favored conservative clothes that kept most of her skin from view while other 16-year-old girls were wearing revealing outfits. Leah spent most of her time in the library researching and reading up on medical advancements. Leah wanted to change the world and hoped to one-day cure cancer, the same disease that had stolen her mother away from her. Leah loved science; she talked about things that Kurt didn't understand. Kurt didn't care; he could sit and listen to Leah talk for days. Her Jamaican accent was hypnotizing, alluring, and seductive. Leah was the most beautiful person Kurt had ever seen. Her beautiful milk chocolate complexion, large brown eyes, and dazzling smile captivated Kurt's heart, but it was her loving, nurturing nature that made him feel safe. Leah naturally cared about everyone, regardless of who they were. To put it mildly, Kurt had a severe crush on Leah. The few years since Kurt had been an honorary member of the Thomas family, his anxiety had never allowed him the courage to ask Leah out on a date. Petrified that if she said no, their friendship would be over, and things would instantly become awkward, so he remained in the dreaded friend zone.

"Ladies and gentlemen," Evelynn's thick Jamaican voice came over the surround sound of Dawn's interrupting Kurt's three-year stroll down memory lane. All forty patrons turned their attention to the hand-carved softwood bar, which Evelynn was now standing on. "Ladies and gentlemen," she repeated to the crowd. "Tonight is not only the beginning of a new year, but it's also the birthday of a close friend of mine. Kurt, come on up."

When Kurt heard his name, his stomach tried to launch its self out of his mouth. Kurt had never enjoyed being the center of attention, no doubt another trait of being a foster child. The mere thought of it made his palms sweat, and his pulse skyrocket. A familiar gravelly voice from inside of Kurt's mind whispered to him.

"You go up there, and you're going to blow chunks all over the place. You know we're right."

"Go on you," Leah whispered in Kurt's ear quietly, having maneuvered through the bar, and the crowd, sneaking up on him. Her breath smelled sweet, no doubt from the champagne she had been illegally drinking through the evening. Kurt may have been turning twenty-one, but Leah had just recently turned nineteen. The sound of her voice immediately calmed Kurt's rapidly increasing pulse. Kurt turned, and she smiled at him.

"Don't keep her waiting," Leah said, placing a loose braid of hair behind her ear nervously. "I have a birthday gift for you too."

Kurt's heart again began to beat exceptionally fast. Leah had never said anything like that to him before. The tone of her voice had a flirty edge to it.

"Boom chic-a pow -wow."

"Kurt! Are you coming?" Evelynn's voice resounded over the bar breaking up Kurt's thoughts about Leah.

Kurt began making his way up to the bar, carefully guiding himself around the intoxicated patrons. At first, everyone had thought that Kurt was a strange young man, but ultimately everyone accepted him after noticing how much the Thomas family cared for him. They all smiled and patted Kurt on the back as he approached Evelynn. Kurt arrived at the bar, where Evelynn reached down and offered Kurt her coconut scented hand as she assisted him up on top of the bar.

"Kurt Bryant," Evelynn said to the crowd. "You are like a son to me. Tonight you turn 21, and well, I just wanted to say happy birthday! You know, me granny on the island always said that a birthday was like a new beginning. You've got to pick yourself up, dust yourself off and start all over again. To new beginnings, and no regrets!" Evelynn said, reaching down for a shot glass of Appleton Estate Jamaican rum and handing it to Kurt. "Drink! Tonight is all about you!"'

"You're going to puke or at least shit yourself in the morning. Don't do it."

Kurt took a deep breath and took the shot glass, and raised it to his mouth. The whole bar grew quiet, watching Kurt as he quickly drank the tepid whiskey. The warm liquid rushed down his throat and punched into his stomach with reckless abandon. As bad as it made him feel, Kurt did his best not to gag. Kurt slammed the glass down, and the bar erupted into cheers.

"This still doesn't make you a man, but never the less, we are impressed."

Kurt had never felt as good as he did at that moment. From the back of the bar, someone began singing happy birthday and the whole bar joined in. From the kitchen, Kurt's best friend Jacob emerged with a cake illuminated by twenty-one candles. Jacob wore a thousand-watt smile on his face as he approached Kurt.

"Appy Birthday, Bredren!"

Kurt was surprised to see Jacob. The last few years had been great for Jacob. He had managed to obtain a full scholarship to run track at Howard University and was currently interning at some important Senators office. Kurt wasn't sure what senator even though Jacob had told him numerous times. People always wondered why Jacob and Kurt were friends since they were opposites. Jacob was an overachiever, while Kurt was deemed lazy. Jacob had gone to college while Kurt still mopped floors and rented a room down the street in a group home. Kurt was introverted and awkward, while Jacob was the life of the party regardless of where he was. Jacob was six foot three and athletic, while Kurt was five foot eleven and built like a video gamer. Jacob was clean-cut and well-groomed, while Kurt had a patchy beard and never combed his thick curly black hair. Jacob was a stud with the ladies while Kurt owned real estate in the friend zone.

"Happy earthsong mi breddah. Mek ah wish!" Jacob said as he lifted the cake in front of his friend.

"Is it just us, or has his accent gotten thicker since he's been interning in D. C.? Bomboclot crazy, he sounds. See, this is what happens when you go to work in Washington; you have to try so hard to fit in and be different at the same time. At least you can understand us even though you try to ignore us most of the time."

Closing his eyes, Kurt wished that this moment would never end. He took a deep breath and blew all the candles out but one. The crowd applauded at the failed attempt.

"Seriously?"

"Who wa cake?" Jacob asked the crowd. He was immediately answered by the bar patrons all at once, making their way towards the cake. "One at a time, one at a time," Jacob cried out.

Kurt couldn't help but laugh as he watched people swarm Jacob for cake. It was a widely known fact around the D. C. area that Dawns was known to have the best dessert in town, thanks mainly to Evelynn and her excellent cooking skills. Someone tapped Kurt on his shoulder. He turned, and Leah was smiling; his stomach responded with an excited lurch.

"Let's get out of here, birthday boy."

"Okay," Kurt answered nervously, hoping that this night would never end.

CHAPTER

L eah and Kurt carefully maneuvered through the cake eating, New Year celebrating, and overall intoxicated crowd and exited through Dawn's back door into the dimly lit alley. A large steel lamp rested over the back street, casting a greenish hue on everything it touched. The light hummed and pulsated, trying its best to withstand the frigid Washington D. C. January weather. The icicles that hung from the power lines sounded like xylophones whenever the wind blew. The blistering arctic front that was currently passing through immediately left exposed skin feeling numb. Leah shivered as the cold air instantly took her breath away; Kurt smiled and wrapped his insulated hooded sweatshirt around her shoulders. The freezing January weather did not affect him.

"Always a gentleman Kurt Bryant," Leah said flirtatiously. "How come you never asked me out, Kurt?"

"Uh... I..." Kurt stuttered.

"Get it together, kid. Now is not the time to forget how to speak."
Leah laughed, "Well, I know you like me, I've known for years, and I think it is cute. Do you want to kiss me? I mean, it is a New year.

Let's start it off right," Leah said, raising her face as close to Kurt's as she could.

Kurt could feel her warm breath against his skin, and he could still smell the sweet champagne. Kurt nervously lowered his face to meet Leah's. A loud crashing noise came from the rear alley, interrupting Kurt's short life's most crucial moment.

"What was that?" Kurt asked Leah.

"I am not sure. Let's go back inside," Leah said, pulling on the door behind Kurt that had closed and automatically locked. "I forgot to flip the deadbolt," Leah said aloud. "Jacob! Mom!" Leah cried out as she banged her fists against the door.

"No one can hear you. There is a party going on," came an unwarranted voice from the shadows.

Leah and Kurt immediately turned to see who had spoken. Standing in a spot that had been vacant a few seconds earlier were three people. It was as if the three had arrived in the bone-chilling wind. The first was a humongous man who stood at least six foot seven and weighed over three hundred pounds. He had a sandy complexion with dark hair and a knotted-looking beard. Even in the dim green lighting, Kurt and Leah could see that his teeth were in horrible shape. The man's teeth were chipped and rotten. The large man had a massive lump in the middle of his back. The man's bulky muscled arms were uneven; the left hung further than the right. The jacket and pants that the man wore were two sizes too small and smelled like rotting trash. The second person was a small skeletal individual dressed in red. A scarlet hoodie covered their head, exposing only the lower half of their bony, wrinkled face. There were what looked like stitches holding the wrinkled flesh to the person's jawbone. This person was in charge; there was a quality of poise and command pouring underneath the scarlet hood.

The third member of the mysterious trio was a woman. The woman's skin looked like fresh snow; it was so white that her jet black hair only magnified her skin's paleness. Her eyes were an intense color of blue that seemed to glow in the darkness. The woman was dressed in what would be politely described as dominatrix chic. Her

5'9 curvaceous body screamed perfection. A black leather catsuit clung to her body so tightly that it looked as if it had been painted on. On each of her exposed forearms were tattoos of large upside-down triangles with a circle pattern of words around each. She looked deadly and enticing at the same time.

"You can't be here," Leah said with nervous authority when she finally stopped staring at the trio and found her voice. "This is private property."

"Oh. Are we interrupting something?" The woman asked as she stepped more into the light. Kurt wasn't sure if it was the dim lighting or the rum that he had drunk, but the triangles that adorned her forearms seemed to be moving.

"See something you like, baby?" the female in black asked Kurt as she crossed the alley with the grace of a lioness.

"The party is inside," Leah said, her voice shaking. The nervous authority now replaced with fear.

"Look like a party here," the behemoth replied in broken English as if he had recently just learned to speak.

"I don't know what you want..." Leah began as she slowly inched closer towards Kurt.

"For you to shut up," the leather-clad woman said, rapidly crossing the alley, striking Leah across the face knocking off her glasses.

Leah instantly fell to the ground holding her face. The behemoth raced over to Kurt and slammed his club-like fist into Kurt's stomach. All the contents in Kurt's stomach introduced themselves to the asphalt before he crumpled to the ground.

"You are not the one we seek, but you will do," the leader in red sneered from underneath his hood.

The behemoth stepped over Kurt's body and picked Leah up by her hair. Leah let out a blood-curdling scream as she struggled while the man dragged her across the icy asphalt. Kurt tried to get up, but he couldn't bring his arms to raise his weight off the ground. Kurt could not recall a time of ever being struck so hard in his life. It felt as if his stomach was protruding out of his back.

"Jacob! Help us!" Leah screamed at the top of her lungs, her voice now holding a desperate edge to it as tears streamed down her terror-stricken face.

"Aww, she is screaming for her big brother. You are supposed to be her knight in shining armor," the leather-clad female said mockingly to Kurt. "Shhh, sweetheart, mummy, and Jacob have their own problems inside."

From inside Dawns, the earlier sounds of music and laughter were suddenly replaced by screams of pain and cries for help. Kurt willed himself enough strength to crawl to the locked back door and managed to sit up, his vision dancing and blurry still. His stomach felt like it was trying to re-inflate itself. Kurt closed his eyes and took a few deep breaths trying to calm his racing heart. Kurt had to try and save Leah from these maniacs. When he opened his eyes, Kurt was surprised at how swiftly the pain waned. From behind Kurt came a thundering noise as the steel backdoor of Dawns exploded off of its hinges. A gust of flames flew from the doorway, reaching up into the night sky. Kurt barely had enough time to roll out of the way of the flying door and the inferno. The steel door unveiled the chaos that was once the happy bar. Bodies were sprawled over the floor, torn apart, and withered. The faces of the bar's patrons were barely recognizable in their disfigurement.

From the bar, a canine-like animal exited. The hefty creature barely fit through the double steel door frame that led from Dawns. The wild beast was the size of a small foreign-made two-seater sports car covered in short, dense black metallic fur. It had an enormous black head with ears that resembled sharpened points. The animal's razor-sharp claws sparked when they crept across the asphalt as the animal moved. With every breath, white frost exited from the creature's nostrils like a steam engine. Kurt's mind instantly transported him back to the night of the fire at Gladys's to the memory of the wolf creature in the hallway. This massive monster that had just exited Dawns had the same black metallic fur as the wolf and the same red intense eyes.

The creature noticed Kurt and snarled ferociously as it hurled itself in his direction. Kurt's reflexes instantly took control as he dodged to the left, grabbed the beast by its hind legs, and slammed it against the brick wall. The creature yelped in pain. Kurt looked down at his hands, wondering how he had acquired such strength and speed.

"*Finally.*"

"Sebastian!" The behemoth cried out, spit flying out of his mouth and catching in his tangled beard. In his outstretched hand, he took Leah by her hair and slammed her to the ground like a ragdoll, her neck snapping as her head smashed against the pavement. The behemoth half charged half shuffled at Kurt, but this time Kurt was prepared. Kurt slid between the large man's legs like a baseball runner, sliding into home plate headfirst. The behemoth, unable to stop his momentum like his pet Sebastian, slammed into the brick wall. Kurt tried to make his way over to Leah, but a recovered Sebastian now blocked his path. The immense beast was baring his razor-sharp teeth at Kurt with cruelty. Large strings of saliva hung from its mouth, pooling on the pavement. The huge man quickly recovered from his blunder and grabbed Kurt by the neck from behind, lifting him with one hand until his toes were barely skimming the ground.

"You watch... then I end you," the man growled. His breath was so intense that Kurt nearly passed out. "Sebastian eats."

The beast turned and headed towards Leah's limp body, its mouth opening wide. Kurt struggled against the giants' grip but to no avail. He was suddenly exhausted. The strength and speed he had recently possessed had dissipated. Sebastian forced himself close to Leah, never taking his haunting red eyes off of Kurt. The animal's mouth opened, and it breathed in and out. A white mist began to rise from Leah's body, and similar to the bodies inside the bar, she began to wither like rotting fruit. Leah's black hair turned grey, her eyes sunk into her skull, and her skin grew tight like plastic all in a matter of seconds.

"No!" Kurt screamed. "Get away from her! I will kill you!"

No sooner had the scream left his lips than the behemoth released Kurt to the cold, wet pavement and clutched his head in pain. The leather-clad woman, the leader in red, and Sebastian grimaced in pain too. The cold flickering lights in the alley all exploded, coating the passage in complete darkness. The shadows illuminated now only by the subzero January moonlight seemed to thrash about as if they were alive, reaching out, encasing everything in sight.

"The freedom we seek is near."

The colossal-sized man dropped to his knees and covered his ears, howling in pain. The pale woman began to hemorrhage from her nose and ears; Sebastian yelped and cowered, a urine line running down his leg. The third mysterious, red-clad person had vanished. As Kurt tried to regain his breath, a set of headlights suddenly pierced the darkness and illuminated the alley with light. The shadows recoiled away from the light receding into the dark corners of the alley. The old, battered sedan barreled down the lane, and Kurt's attackers threw themselves inside the vehicle. Kurt had only a moment to roll out of the way of the sedan as it sped off.

Just like that, they were all gone, and Kurt was alone again, surrounded by the dark silence and death. Exhausted, Kurt managed to drag himself over to Leah, who he was nervously trying to kiss some five minutes ago. Kurt lay beside Leah and turned her over and instantly felt his heart shatter. The body that lay before him wasn't that of a healthy nineteen-year-old girl. This body should have been on display at an Egyptian exhibit. Leah's body was old and worn, her eyes were sunken in, and her thick black hair was now thin and grey. As Kurt knelt over Leah and placed a kiss on her forehead, a powerful blast exploded from within Dawns. The explosion propelled Kurt across the alley, slamming him into a brick wall where the back of his head absorbed most of the impact. As Kurt lay on the cold pavement, his arms outstretched, reaching for Leah, her body a few feet away from him, he succumbed to the pain and lost consciousness.

CHAPTER

3

The nightmares came and went in waves. Kurt struggled to survive the rush of horrors that invaded his sleep. Scenes from the alley kept repeating themselves vividly in his mind. In his nightmares, Kurt tried his hardest to save Leah, but the outcome never changed. No matter what he did, Leah always ended up with the same fate, devoured by Sebastian. In his nightmares, Kurt sensed something else was in the alley with him. It was powerful, ancient, and angry. It scared Kurt more than the trio he had encountered, but it also put him at ease. When Kurt finally awoke nine days later from his nightmares, he immediately did not recognize his surroundings.

Kurt was lying on a cot in what seemed to be a small six-by-eight storage room with intense, tangerine-colored walls. Beside his cot was a wobbly nightstand with three rickety legs that looked like it belonged in a dumpster. The rest of the décor also kept with the same dumpster chic theme. The thick plaid blankets that covered him were old and worn; the stench of mothballs and baking soda still clung to them. Bags of potatoes lined the adjacent wall of the small room. Twenty-one unlabeled cans of food were lined neatly in a row on a makeshift plywood bookshelf next to the potatoes. There were old milk crates in the far corner full of vegetables, some of which were moldy and starting to smell. An old freezer hummed loudly in the corner, a puddle of water beginning to pool underneath the outdated appliance. Kurt quietly got up from his cot, surprised that his body wasn't sore at all.

Kurt remembered slamming into the brick wall before he lost consciousness, yet there was no lump on the back of his head. Maybe he hadn't hit the wall as hard as he thought. Kurt looked down at his clothes; they were torn and covered in blood. Kurt wasn't sure whose blood it was, but he was optimistic that it wasn't his. Kurt decided it would be best to escape his tangerine-colored prison. Who knew what fate waited for him if he stayed. Kurt crossed the room and cautiously tested the door handle. To his surprise, the handle turned. Kurt opened the door and peered out. The delicious smell hit him first, causing his stomach to growl. Someone was baking a homemade apple pie. Kurt told himself to relax and made his way from his resting place. In front of Kurt was a warped-looking staircase leading up. Knowing he did not have a lot of time to waste, Kurt cautiously bounded up the stairs, his nervous heartbeat mimicking his quick steps.

The staircase emptied into a kitchen that had the same tangerine color walls as the storage room. Kurt scanned the dated kitchen. There was an old wood-burning stove that looked like it belonged in a different era. The refrigerator across the room was also an antique, but at least it was from this century. The old refrigerator made a loud droning noise as if someone was continuously hitting the motor with a wrench. Kurt looked to his left and noticed several knives on the counter and quickly armed himself with the sharpest one. He wasn't sure if a knife could hurt the large man or Sebastian, but he much rather die trying to protect himself. From across the room, Kurt heard someone approaching the kitchen. Kurt quickly raced across the room and slid behind the door just as it opened. A young man entered the room carrying a tray of dishes. He was white, fresh-faced, skinny, and had a haircut that resembled a lopsided seagull. Kurt wasted no time; he grabbed the intruder from behind and placed his newly acquired knife to his throat.

"Make a sound, and I will kill you," Kurt told him nervously. He had never hurt anyone in his entire life, but Kurt knew that he needed to be prepared to act after the events in the alley. The young man responded by fearfully dropping his tray of plates to the floor with a loud crash.

"Son of a bitch!" Kurt said, knowing the loud commotion would bring others to see what happened. Kurt grabbed the emo teenager by the collar of his hipster labeled t-shirt and hauled him to the top of the warped staircase.

Kurt again placed the knife firmly to the boys' throat and snarled. "Move, and you're dead."

A slim blond teenage girl adorned in a ratty grey t-shirt, and black pants with holes over the knees appeared mere seconds after the noise.

"Trevor, are you alright in here, you dipshit?" she began. Seeing Kurt with a knife to her friend's throat, the girl started screaming at the top of her lungs. Kurt tightened his grip on the kitchen knife, his hands now clammy and shaking with uneasiness.

The girls' screams were answered by the rapid approaching sound of shuffling feet. It sounded like a whole army was coming to her rescue. Kurt took a deep breath and prepared himself for Sebastian, and whoever else would join him. Three small elderly women entered the kitchen. Each woman was wearing an ankle-length denim skirt and a white short-sleeve button-up shirt. The shirts were embroidered with an outline of a dove flying over a rainbow over the left front pocket. These women were followed by a middle-aged man dressed in all black who also sported the same dove and rainbow logo. Behind him was what looked like a crowd of dirty, unkempt homeless men and women. One of the older women grabbed the blond female while keeping her eyes on Kurt and began to comfort her.

"Shhh, Savannah, it will be okay. Did he hurt you?"

Savannah did not answer them because she was still in the process of screaming.

"No, I didn't hurt her, but could you please shut her up?" Kurt appealed as he tightened his grip on the dish boy.

"Savannah, dear, calm down," the black-clad man said before turning his attention to Kurt. "Son, let's be reasonable. Put the knife down and let Trevor go free."

"Yeah, right," Kurt replied, tightening his grip on Trevor's collar. "So your giant friend and his life force-draining pet dog can get me. I don't think so."

"He must be high," one of the homeless men said from the door.

"I am not high," Kurt replied. "I have seen some shit that I can't explain, though."

"Sounds high to me," another of the homeless men responded. The others nodded in agreement. "Probably on those millennial bath salts."

"Listen, son, put the knife down. Do we look like we work for a giant that has a pet who can eat you?" The man in black asked as he took another step closer to Kurt.

Kurt had to admit, the group in front of him didn't look like they worked with the trio from the alley. Scanning the leathery-faced man in front of him, Kurt placed his age between forty –five and fifty with a graying Caesar haircut and a tanned, rugged face. The man looked as if he had been in a few fights in his life, there was a deep scar over his left eye, and his nose slanted at a downward angle. No doubt it had been broken a time or two. Underneath the all-black outfit, Kurt thought he could make out the remains of muscles, which now had been replaced with flab. The three elderly women were at least twenty-five years older than the man in black. Two of the women wore bifocals, and one did not. All three women had drooping cheeks that reminded Kurt of an old cartoon hound dog detective. Sensing that Kurt was relaxing, the man continued to speak.

"You are in a soup kitchen at New Beginnings Church in Richmond, Virginia. I am Pastor Elias Manningham, and you are," the black-clad man asked Kurt as he extended his hand.

The man's hand seemed harmless enough, but Kurt noticed that the man's knuckles were bruised and scarred, validating Kurt's deduction that this man was once a fighter.

"Confused," Kurt replied as he let Trevor go and handed Elias the knife.

CHAPTER

"And that is all I remember," Kurt said over a brown lunch tray that contained two stale peanut butter sandwiches and two scoops of homemade potato salad. Kurt's stomach was growling, but revisiting the night of the murder of his friends had caused him to lose his appetite. Kurt stared at the food as he explained to Elias Manningham the events that had occurred on what he believed to be the night before.

"Well, son, New Year's day was nine days ago," Elias started.

The two were sitting at an elementary school-style cafeteria table with multi-colored stools in a large room. The room walls were painted the same tangerine color as the storage room that Kurt awoke in. Members of the homeless occupied the other twenty tables, looking for what would most likely be their only meal of the day. Judging by the room's tangerine decor, Kurt assumed that New Beginnings Church was once an old Mexican restaurant or small manufacturing office. There were still faint outlines where old machinery or restaurant equipment once lined the walls. The lights in the room flickered and buzzed loudly. Moldy ceiling tiles bulged with water, ready to burst at any moment. There were buckets strategically placed around the room to catch droplets of water drizzling down from the ceiling. The smell of mold was strong, and the attempt to cover the scent with Pine-Sol only made the mold smell that much more apparent. The room's noise level was deafening; everyone was talking about the events of the morning. Elias moved around the table to sit closer to Kurt.

"The internet says an electrical fire was the cause of the fire at Dawns. Unfortunately, there were no survivors," Elias said, showing Kurt the article on his phone.

"Electrical fire was not the cause, at least not this time. I told you, a giant man, a leather broad, some old skeleton person in a red robe, and a giant hell beast attacked us. You think I am crazy, don't you? Everyone always thinks I'm crazy."

"No, son, I do not."

"Why not?" Kurt asked dejectedly; he hardly believed the story himself, and he had been there.

"Kurt, how do you think you got from Washington D. C to Richmond? I drove you," Elias said, not giving Kurt a chance to answer. "I was in Washington D.C. I tried to reach my congressional representative regarding a grant for our church that was submitted months ago. As you can see, this place is not in the best of shape. After an unexciting meeting with my representative, who was none too happy I visited his home on New Year's Eve. I ruined his celebration with a woman who wasn't his spouse. After being removed somewhat forcefully by security, I got back in my car and prepared to head back to Richmond. I had barely gotten on the road when the snow started coming down in sheets. I thought about turning around and trying to find a cheap hotel. I am not a man with a vast fortune, so I decided to push on. Fortunately, I was the only vehicle on the road. As I was nearing the interstate, you appeared out of thin air right in front of my car. I tried to slow down, but in the snow, the ice, and the fact that my car is desperate for a brake job, the impact was definite. I slammed into you so hard that you flew over the roof of my car. I thought I had killed you. I stopped the car to check on you, but you were already getting back up. You were covered in blood, but you seemed to heal right before my eyes. You looked at me and kept saying she's gone, she's gone, and then you collapsed in the snow. I dragged you to my car, and I brought you here. I didn't know what to do. I just panicked."

Kurt stared at Elias for a moment before speaking. "So let me get this straight, you hit me with a car and decided to bring me to Richmond? You seemed to heal before my eyes," Kurt said, mimicking Elias's voice. "Give me a break, my guy. I'm not sure what your angle is but count me out," Kurt said, anger rising in his voice, causing the room once filled with chatter to go quiet.

Elias looked down at his hands before standing up and staring Kurt in his eyes. "I am sorry if I upset you. I was only trying to help. I thought of calling the authorities, but I didn't know how to explain what had happened. Besides, with my records involving DUI's, I'm sure the authorities would've assumed I had been drinking. Which I had not been. I could've left you in the street, and when the authorities arrived, I do not doubt that you would've led them back to your charred friends. Do you think the police would've believed your story? I believe it, and yet I still can't believe it. So please stop with the self-righteous act and see my point of view. It's better to be here than being under a four-hundred-pound sweaty man in jail. As angry and tough as you feel now, let's be honest; you're too pretty for jail."

"Damn, this guy is just spitting out facts right now. Stop being so ungrateful and self-righteous."

Kurt hated to admit this, but both the voices in his head and Elias were right. Kurt wasn't very good at apologizing, but he gave a half-hearted apology without apologizing, knowing he was wrong.

"I'm kind of glad that you didn't call the police. One peak in my foster file and they would've assumed that I started the fire. Once I told them what happened, you're right; they would've locked me up somewhere and pumped me full of crazy pills. I would've been better off dying at Dawns," Kurt said, covering his face trying to hide his tears. "I have to get back to D. C. and figure out what to do next."

"No, I don't think that's a good idea," Elias said, placing his hand on his chin. "What if you're supposed to be here? What if we're supposed to help each other?"

"I wouldn't have needed your help if you hadn't hit me with a car," Kurt said sarcastically.

"Well, that was quick."

"Hear me out, as I said, I ran into you with my car, yet you have no injuries," Elias continued ignoring Kurt's rude interjection. "What if divine intervention brought us together."

"Like some magic deity murdered my friends, had me jumped in the alley, and then got me hit by what I imagine is a mid-sized older model sedan," Kurt replied, looking down at the tread pattern on his torn pants. "Couldn't this deity call down from the clouds and just tell me to get my ass to Richmond."

"You wouldn't listen anyway. We've been talking to you since you can remember."

"Kurt, I believe that you're special. As I said, I saw you heal before my eyes. I feel that there's more at work than we know. I would like you to remain here and help me. You have no reason to trust me. You have nowhere to go, and I'm offering you shelter," Elias said, getting up from the table and walking towards the door behind him, urging Kurt to follow, which he reluctantly did. "Young man, I wouldn't be doing my duty as a pastor if I didn't properly offer you guidance. Please forgive me for what happens next," Elias said as he pulled the knife Kurt used an hour ago on Trevor out of his back pocket and plunged it deep into Kurt's chest.

Kurt gasped in disbelief. All the shit he'd been through nine days ago fighting an imitation goth warrior princess in black leather, facing a foreign car-sized dog, and a man built like a small tank. Was this how it was going to end, stabbed in the chest by a washed-up born-again pastor in a dirty mold-infested kitchen in Richmond, Virginia.

CHAPTER

The first thing that Kurt realized was that getting stabbed hurt like hell, but the pain didn't last more than a few seconds. Kurt stumbled back a few steps and fell to one knee, the knife still sticking from his chest. Taking a deep breath, Kurt grabbed the blade's hilt and pulled it out in one swift motion. The knife made a sloshing sound as it reversed its course from out of Kurt's chest. To Kurt's surprise, there was very little blood on the blade or himself. Kurt pulled himself up from the floor and placed the knife in the trash. Kurt watched in amazement as the knife wound instantly began to repair itself. The hole in Kurt's chest became whole again in a few seconds, like a time-elapsed film played in reverse.

"Dick move. What if you had been wrong?"

"I had to show you I wasn't crazy. I'm glad this worked out the way it did," Elias said apprehensively.

"You weren't positive that I wouldn't die before you stabbed me?

"I was positive you were special, but I didn't know to what degree," Elias explained to Kurt.

"Like when the big guy hit me in the alley," Kurt said aloud, only hearing half of what Elias was saying. "One moment, I was bent over, my stomach deflated by his punch, then the next moment, I was fine. I could have saved Leah, Jacob, and everyone in Dawns, but I was scared."

The memories of the screams echoing from Dawns as Sebastian slaughtered his friends began to overtake Kurt's consciousness. Sensing that Kurt was blaming himself, Elias spoke gently.

"They may be gone physically, but they live on spiritually. Come on; let's go back to my office."

"No!" Kurt replied with blatant aggression in his voice. "I have to find who hurt my friends. Now that I can do this, things will be different. I don't have time to find myself with you".

"Son, I promise I will do everything I can to help you, but we must talk first. Please."

Kurt sighed unenthusiastically and again followed Elias from the kitchen through the banquet room and upstairs to his office. The upstairs of the church was in worse shape than the downstairs, if that was imaginable. The peeling paint on the walls exposed the warped drywall and stairs that were mostly dry rotted. The stairs bent ominously as Kurt and Elias ascended. The last three stairs were gone entirely; Kurt had to leap over the hole in the ground to make it to the second floor. Kurt wasn't a structural engineer, but he was sure the city inspector should think about condemning this building. Kurt tried not to stare at the black moldy ceiling tiles as he entered Elias's office. The room was small and sparingly furnished with second-hand tables and lamps. Kurt was surprised to see the medals that covered the walls.

"One bronze in the Junior Olympics and a couple of amateur titles," Elias said to Kurt with a nonchalant shrug. "I've boxed since I was seven years old, have a seat." Elias motioned to a worn leather chair across from his desk as he too took a seat, "I am sure right now you have more questions that I don't have answers for, but obstacles are placed in our paths to make us stronger. Everything happens for a reason."

"Yeah, I have a few questions. First, what type of church is this, and why does it smell like the inside of a moldy closet. Secondly, how does one become a former priest?"

"And people say we're rude assholes."

Elias looked at Kurt, bothered by the young man's bluntness, but he didn't let Kurt's rudeness rattle him. "This building may not look the best, but it provides help and hope to its parishioners. Those who come here seek guidance, and we try to help them. This building isn't much, but it's more than enough. I purchased this building and the two adjacent plots at a city foreclosure auction. I planned on renovating them both, but money has been hard to come by due to the economy. People aren't willing to donate money when they barely have enough money to get by themselves, and the government isn't handing out many grants these days. To answer the second rude question, I was a priest in the Catholic Church before my time here. I had a congregation that numbered into the hundreds, but I was not happy. Over time I noticed how stubborn the church was. Even though the world is constantly changing, the church's beliefs stayed the same. So I left and started my own church, a place where all are welcome regardless of who or what you believe."

"What about the old women who follow you around? Did they come with the building, or did you recruit them to work in this hope-giving establishment?" Kurt asked cynically. "And no offense, I think, I'm going to call you Padre. Is that cool?"

"Two of the women are former nuns that served with me in my past profession. They are still called Sisters. Even though they resigned the title, everyone still considers them nuns, and as I told you earlier, you can call me whatever you feel like you need to call me. A title doesn't define a man; his actions are what define him."

"This guy is deep, or either he's full of a lot of shit."

"Do you have any more questions regarding what you have learned about yourself?" Elias asked Kurt, who was leaned back in his chair, staring at the water spot in the ceiling above him.

"I have a ton of questions, most of them you probably can't answer. I mean, can I survive a fall from space? Can I hold my breath underwater? Am I ever going to grow old and die?" Kurt said, crossly trying to cover his indistinctness about his new situation.

"I understand your confusion and your questions, but the only way to get answers is to test your abilities. I am fairly sure your body does more things than just heal. Would you like to see what else you can do?"

"What do you have in mind?"

"Can I ask a favor of you? You have every right to say no?"

"Well, it depends on what it is. I know you priests ask strange things from young boys. Hopefully, I am too old for your taste."

"Oh, that was a good one. Perhaps there's hope for you yet."

"I have a friend who needs our help. I understand you are still reeling from your loss, but perhaps you could find it in your heart to help me."

Kurt considered the request for a moment. He was alone and had no place to go, and above all else, he felt lost. "Sure. Why not Padre? I'm sure it can't be that bad, right?"

CHAPTER

"Sure, why not? It can't be that bad right," Kurt said aloud. "I know I am not from around here, but that looks like a crack house."

The building that Kurt was looking at was an abandoned warehouse that stood in the middle of a vacant lot. Once, it had been an integral part of the community, which like the warehouse, also had taken a turn for the worse. This particular area of town had once been the heart of the city, but cutbacks and cheap labor from other countries were responsible for the decline. People lost their jobs first, then their community to crime and drugs, and finally, they lost their spirits. The warehouse now mirrored the general tone of the city, run-down, neglected, and forgotten.

For the past hour, Kurt and Elias had been parked down the block from the abandoned warehouse. Kurt had counted forty-seven people going into the building and none coming out. Three men guarded the only entrance, and at the moment, all three were huddled around a barrel that had a fire going inside of it.

"Who could you possibly know in there? Is there a drug-dealing nun that owes you money that you want me to collect from?" Kurt asked.

"My goddaughter Michelle is in there. Her parents died last May. She met this guy called Spider shortly after she moved into the church. It is a known fact that Spider is a drug dealer, but Michelle wouldn't listen," Elias said miserably with a look of both pain and concern etched into his facial features.

"How old is she, Padre?"

"Nineteen," Elias replied, pulling a picture from his wallet and handing it to Kurt.

Kurt took the photograph from Elias's hand and looked at the girl in the picture. Kurt felt a wave of jealousy flood over him. The girl in the photo was smiling; her eyes were full of life. Kurt remembered Leah and how she looked withered and dead against the icy pavement that night. Her youth and beauty drained from her body. Kurt had to fight back against a wave of nausea and tears as the nightmarish memory continued to flash through his mind.

"And you moved her into a church? Man, you were asking for it. Stay here, and keep the car running. We may need to leave in a hurry," Kurt said, getting out of the car swiftly, not wanting Elias to see him getting emotional.

"Wait! What are you going to do? Spider isn't the type of guy to just let Michelle go with a stranger," Elias called after Kurt.

"Nice to know; at least I can't die right," Kurt said to himself as he approached the building. He was eager to test the limits of his abilities. He may have failed to save his friends, but maybe he could rescue this girl.

Kurt pulled the green hood of his borrowed sweatshirt from one of the many left in the church's donation box over his head. Kurt looked at the picture and saved the image into his mind. Michelle was tanned, petite, with rust-colored hair. The picture showed that she had a few blue streaks of colored hair on the right side. Her hair was chin-length and cut into a bob. Kurt committed the photo to his mind and placed the borrowed picture in his tattered jeans' back pocket. Kurt closed his eyes and took a deep breath of preparation as he approached the warehouse.

Something awoke inside of Kurt, something ancient, savage, and undeniably evil from an unfathomable place. Kurt felt the strange power reach down to the very depth of his soul. Suddenly he wanted to terminate anything that was in his way. The sudden surge of energy within Kurt felt extremely pleasurable. Underneath his hood, Kurt's eyes turned black as if they were filled with liquid coal.

"Finally, we have waited years for this moment. Allow us to baptize you into the fold."

In front of the building, the three guards were gathered around a small fire burning inside an old discarded barrel. The three men were all huge, former high school or collegiate offensive linemen in another life. Their giant hands all held out in front of them, being warmed by the fire. Each of them wore black hats with the same logo, 804 embroidered over the shape of Virginia. All three men looked to be in their early twenties. One was Hispanic, and the other two black, one being a very light complexion like Kurt. The Hispanic man craned his neck when he caught a glimpse of Kurt approaching. He quickly made the visitor known to the other two, and the three men turned to face the advancing stranger.

"Yo, you lost dog?" one of the guards called to Kurt as he approached.

Kurt didn't answer. He continued on his path toward the entrance of the drug house. He did not even spare a glance in the direction of the guards.

"Yo, asshole. Hold up, didn't you hear us talking to you?" Another guard yelled at Kurt stepping in front of him in an attempt to block his path.

"I don't want any trouble. I'm here for a friend," Kurt hissed from under his hood, trying to resist the terrible urge of making this man beg for his life.

"Give into the temptation. You will feel so much better, we promise. Let us guide you through this introductory lesson of distributing pain."

"I'm not your friend, but I can introduce you to an ass-kicking," the guard replied as he pulled out a pair of brass knuckles from his pocket. The other two guards followed suit and armed themselves with various weapons of their own, a baseball bat and a knife, respectively.

Under the hood, Kurt sneered. These men were willing to die to protect this warehouse, and at the moment, Kurt was happy to oblige them. Kurt clinched his fist and sprang into action. All the pent-up frustration of not saving Leah was unleashed, not to mention the release of demonic adrenaline that now coursed through his body. Kurt's mind cried out for the destruction of these three men. Mr. Brass Knuckles threw a right punch that Kurt stopped in the palm of his hand. Kurt sadistically smiled as he squeezed with his newly acquired strength, pulverizing every bone in the guard's hand. Kurt flung the man into the wall as if he weighed three pounds, knocking him unconscious. The guard with the baseball bat seeing his friend in trouble, swung at Kurt's head. Kurt ducked quickly, and the guard's momentum carried him into a 180-degree rotation exposing his back. Kurt caught the guard with a perfectly placed punch in the lower portion of his back. The sound of the man's spine snapping in half reverberated through the air. The man went limp and fell face down on the pavement, his body not moving. The guard with the knife stared at Kurt with disbelief. Kurt could practically taste the fear rolling off of this man in waves. It was euphoric.

"P.. P.. Please," the guard begged. "Don't hurt me!"

Kurt smirked underneath the borrowed hood, the fear was like a drug, and he wanted more.

"*Kill him.*"

"How many people have you hurt with that knife, and be honest? We will know if you lie." Kurt asked as he approached the petrified guard. "Tell us."

The guard's lip started to tremble, "I only do what I am told. Please don't hurt me."

"Answer the question!"

"Two people. I've only cut two people, but just to scare them, I swear."

"That is two too many," Kurt growled, pouncing on the guard. Kurt took the knife and made two quick slashing motions, carving two large gouges in each of the man's cheeks. The weight of the man's facial flesh pulled on the two cuts until it was possible to see the faint glimmer of white bone through the wall of blood that flowed from the facial wounds. Kurt had cut the man so severely that his teeth and gums were visible through the hanging flesh. Kurt's victim fell to the ground clutching his ruined visage and letting out an agonizing scream of shock and pain before passing out.

"We admit we are impressed. Death would've been better, but not bad for your first time. You always remember your first time."

"Now you'll think twice before doing what you're told," Kurt smiled evilly from under the borrowed sweatshirt as he entered the drug house, his eyes still radiating black as he looked back, admiring the destruction he had created.

CHAPTER

E lias said a silent prayer for the three young men he just witnessed Kurt tear through from his stakeout spot one block away. He was tempted to drive from his location and check on the men, but he didn't want to jeopardize the rescue of his goddaughter Michelle. Was it selfish? Was it the wrong thing to do? Elias couldn't put the life of his goddaughter at any additional risk. Kurt was the only one who could get her out of Spider's clutches. Elias slumped down in the driver's seat of his sedan and looked away from the three men lying on the ground. "It will be ok. It just looks worse than it is."

CHAPTER

Kurt entered the uninhibited warehouse and submerged himself in darkness. The only light illuminating through the abandoned warehouse was from the setting sun that crept through the boarded-up windows. The scents that were confined in the building were inebriating. Sweat, blood, and tears mixed with abandonment, desperation, and hopelessness. Cloaked in the darkness of the building, Kurt felt as though he was one with all the suffering.

"Bask in this newfound glory. Gorge yourself on the misery and the anguish."

The ungodly power continued to surge through Kurt's entire body. His senses were more acute than ever. He heard everything down to the most silent of sounds. This increased power also allowed Kurt to see through the darkness that had now overcome the entire building. Kurt navigated through the murkiness as if he were a part of it. Piled to one side of the massive open warehouse were discarded machinery and factory equipment. Addiction occupied the rest of the room. Stepping over crack pipes and other paraphernalia, Kurt silently maneuvered through the warehouse, stopping to look at the resting bodies slumped on the floor. Intertwined, their desire to get high was the only thing that weighed on their dependent minds. Kurt could smell the despondency that rose from the bodies like an errant stench, which excited him. Kurt got as close as he dared without causing any of the unconscious addicts to stir. He didn't see Michelle in the group of addicts, so he continued, but not before he took a deep breath of desperation and smiled.

"So are we on a scavenger hunt? It's nice to see you using us to our full potential."

Kurt elected to make his way upstairs. The stairs creaked and groaned underneath his weight. When Kurt arrived at the second level, he saw that this level was livelier than the one downstairs. Addicts were in the process of shooting up and servicing one another. Lost in their self-induced paradise of pain, no one paid Kurt any attention as he watched from the shadows. They were oblivious to everything except the need to get high. From the end of the hall, Kurt heard a baby crying. There could be no good reason that a baby was in a place like this. Kurt himself knew firsthand what it felt like to be abandoned as a child, but as bad as his childhood was, it didn't involve drug house visits. Kurt silently ran his fingers against the wall as he walked towards the sound of the crying baby; thick flakes of paint fell to the floor like a trail of led-laced bread crumbs.

Kurt peered into the room where he discovered a jaundiced colored teenage girl no older than eighteen trying to trade her newborn daughter to a man with a spider tattoo on his neck. The girl wore her blond hair in two messy, uneven pigtails. Burn marks littered her private school green and black checkered skirt. Tied in a knot above her midriff with the top three buttons undone, she wore a filthy white button-down long sleeve oxford shirt. One of her green knee highs was missing, and the other hung around her ankle torn. Her zombie-like appearance and yellow-tinged skin made her look like a sixty-five-year-old cosplaying as a drug-addicted school girl. The olive-skinned man with the spider tattoo on his neck was maybe five-eight, with spiked dark hair. Multiple piercings lined the right side of his face, one in his eyebrow, one in his nose, and an industrial piercing running through his ear's upper cartilage. A pencil-thin mini douche bag beard ran the length of his jawline. On a seedy-looking couch in the corner sat four men and Michelle. Kurt merged into the shadows as he listened.

"Please, all I need is one hit. Spider, please give me what I need. Here, you can have Amber," the teenage mother begged, trying to hand her baby to Spider.

"What the fuck do I want with your baby?" Spider asked rudely.

"A crack baby at that," one of the four men chimed in from the tattered old couch. The other three men on the sofa roared with laughter.

"Please, Spider, you know I can do things to you Michelle can't do," the teenager continued seductively.

"Are you serious? We've had our fun, I got you high, and you ended up dropping out of school and had a baby. All that private school money is gone, and what do you have to show for it? You thought you were so much better than me. Now, look at you, begging me to give you another hit."

"Spider, please leave her alone," Michelle whimpered from the couch.

Michelle looked nothing like the picture Kurt had in his back pocket. Her skin seemed gray and stretched over her bony cheeks, and her eyes seemed empty and hollow. The once vibrant young woman looked as if she too had aged twenty years in the few months she had been gone.

"Shut up! When I want your opinion, I'll give it to you. At least this bitch knows what a man wants," Spider sneered angrily.

The baby, who had been quiet for a few minutes, began to cry again. The screams were high-pitched and loud. The baby was undoubtedly in indescribable pain, each moment of her new life struggling through painful drug withdrawal, thanks to her mother and the man who supplied her. Kurt's anger boiled over from the shadows; underneath his hood, his eyes blazed black with rage. Kurt moved from his hiding place in the shadows and relocated behind the wall where the four men and Michelle sat on the couch.

"I guess I could give you one more hit for old times sake," Kurt heard Spider say.

"*Heard enough yet? If you don't get in there, that girl will be expecting again in nine months. Does the world need another drug-addicted baby?*"

The evil power flowing within Kurt had to be released. Kurt punched through the wall with ease, grabbing two of the four men on the couch by the back of their collars, pulling them through the wall, and flinging them over the stairs. The men screamed as they fell through the air, their arms flailing as they landed on a pile of addicts some sixty feet below. Kurt quickly disposed of the other two with ease by beating their skulls against each other. Neither moved after that, either dead or unconscious, Kurt did not care which. Kurt entered through the wall, his clothing now covered with old drywall and dust. Standing in the middle of the room were Spider and the teenage mother. Michelle remained on the couch, her eyes darting back and forth, unsure of what to do. The crying baby rested on the floor, unwanted like trash.

"What the fuck, asshole? Do you want to die?" Spider asked.

"Do you?" Kurt growled, crossing the room and kicking Spider square in his crotch.

"*Two points!*"

Spider went down in a heap of pain, crying, and screaming profanities. Numerous voices answered Spider's shouts. Downstairs the sleeping addicts raced up the stairs to their fallen supplier.

Kurt glared at the teenage girl as he pulled his hood back, exposing his blacked-out eyes. "Pick up your baby and leave. I won't give you a second chance. Go home and raise your child or die today with this waste. The choice is yours. If I ever catch you here again, you will be very sorry. Now get out of here before I change my mind about your mothering skills."

The teenage girl wasted no time gathering her child; she never took her eyes off the black-eyed monster except to cast a fleeting glance at Michelle.

"She will be okay. Now move!" Kurt barked as the teenage girl fled.

"*She will win a Nobel prize one day. Sike. Do people still say sike?*"

Kurt turned toward Michelle, who backed away in fear when she saw how black his eyes were. "I'm not going to hurt you. Elias sent me to get you out of here," Kurt explained softly, "Just stay close."

Kurt extended his hand toward her. Michelle was terrified but at the same time comforted by his words. She grabbed his hand, and Kurt pulled his hood back over his face. At that moment, Spider's addicts and remaining crew burst into the room and saw him on the ground, still screaming in pain. They had never witnessed this before and had no idea what to do.

"Don't just stand there!" Spider screamed, "Fuck him up!"

No one advanced towards the dust-covered man with the hood over his face.

"Whoever puts this punk out of his misery gets high for free for the next year," Spider groaned.

All at once, the crowd of thirty-three men and women charged the stranger in the room. Kurt moved fast; his newfound powers guided his fist with precision. Kurt worked with whatever he was given and made sure that the attackers wished they hadn't gotten out of bed that morning. Parrying blows and striking in vital areas, Kurt quickly disposed of the addicts. The sounds of bones breaking and the screams of agony were like music to Kurt's ears. Kurt could've easily killed his attackers, but he decided to go easy on them. Their addictions were no reason for them to die.

"*You're no fun at all. If we killed them, we'd be freeing them from their addiction, duh.*"

"Say goodbye because we're leaving," Kurt said, pulling Michelle along towards the door.

Spider watched in disbelief. In a span of a few minutes, he'd been dethroned and embarrassed. "Go with him then. You are a useless whore anyway!" Spider screamed after Michelle as she made her way to the door with the stranger. "You'll be back, you stupid bitch! You will be back!"

"*This fool does not fear or respect us. We should give him a lesson in both.*"

Kurt stopped in his tracks. "On second thought, we'll take the window."

CHAPTER

E lias was getting nervous. It had been fifteen minutes since
Kurt had gone into the abandoned warehouse. Five minutes
had passed since he heard the screams from inside. Elias debated
calling the police. Elias had worked hard to build up New Beginnings
Church, and his being present at a known drug house would not be
becoming for the church's image. There would be no explanation that
he could give to explain his stakeout position. The lack of movement
from within the warehouse led Elias to believe that Kurt may have
been in trouble. It wasn't a good idea to send the young man inside
when who knew what waited for him. Elias decided that if Kurt and
Michelle were in trouble, it was up to him to help them. Elias started
up his battered blue 2000 Ford Taurus and put it into drive. He had
barely touched the gas pedal when someone flew from one of the
windows. Elias watched, horrified as the man crashed into a pile of
wooden pallets some seventy feet below. Elias pulled his car into the
parking lot and got out to check on the fallen figure.

"Spider?" Elias said aloud, glancing down at the black widow
tattooed on the fallen young man's neck. Fearing the worst, he bent

down and checked for a pulse. A wave of relief overtook him as he found one.

"Heads up!"

Elias barely had a chance to move before Kurt landed beside him, carrying an unconscious Michelle. Elias stepped away in fear noticing that Kurt's eyes blazed black with ferocity.

"See how this one shows us the ultimate respect. His fear is his gratitude."

"Don't sweat it," Kurt said, noticing Elias's concern. "I have this under control."

Closing his eyes, Kurt used a technique he used to help control his anxiety. Kurt took several deep breaths and counted to ten, forcing himself to relax. The dark power that had been surging through Kurt's body subsided. Kurt opened his eyes and stared at Elias. His eyes reverted to normal.

"Let's get out of here," Elias said to Kurt stepping over Spider's unconscious body. "We don't want to be here when he wakes up."

Smiling, Kurt too stepped over Spider's limp body as he headed to the idling car. "I bet this gives new meaning to the term coming down from a high," Kurt joked.

"Boom, roasted!"

Elias smiled nervously and looked around at the chaos that he had helped unleash. There were four victims outside, and who knew how many more were inside. The guards that Kurt had dispatched earlier were still lying on the ground, not moving. The former priest said a small prayer under his breath as he got into his old car.

"Forgive me for what I have done. I only wanted Michelle to return to me safely. What other choice did I have?"

CHAPTER

Article from the Richmond Main Street Gazette

Next week, the Legendary Codex Gigas will be here in Richmond at the Virginia Museum of Fine Arts (VMFA). The priceless artifact on loan from The National Library of Sweden in Stockholm will be the main attraction as the museum prepares to reopen after its multi-million dollar renovations. The Codex Gigas is the most extensive existing medieval manuscript in the world. Thought to have been created in the early twelfth century, this exhibit is expected to draw huge crowds while here in Richmond.

Dubbed the Devil's Bible due to the large illustration on the inside and the legend of its creation, the Codex Gigas tale is one that Hollywood itself couldn't fabricate. According to legend, the scribe was a monk who broke his monastic vows and was sentenced to be walled up alive. To forbear his harsh penalty, the monk promised to create a book to glorify his monastery, including all human knowledge in one single night. Near midnight it became clear that his task wouldn't be completed. The scribe made a special prayer to the devil, asking for help. In exchange for assistance in completing the book, the writer would sacrifice his soul willingly to hell. When guards checked the next morning, the monk had somehow vanished from his locked cell, and the book was completed. According to modern-day testing, scientists have confirmed that one author completed the Codex Gigas but would have taken the average person forty years to complete.

The lore of The Codex Gigas is one of the main reasons for its popularity. Museum officials expect over five hundred thousand visitors to the Virginia Museum of Fine Arts while The Codex Gigas is on display. Tickets for this exhibit are on sale now and are expected to sell out. Museum enthusiasts have been camping out for weeks to get a glance at this legendary work of art. Tickets are $85.00 for nonmembers of the VMFA and free for those who have purchased an annual membership. The city of Richmond is expected to take in several million dollars of revenue from this exhibit while it is here, which will help aid the city's struggling economy.

CHAPTER

After arriving back at New Beginnings Church, Elias took Michelle upstairs to rest and left Kurt alone to his own devices. Kurt's stomach growled uncontrollably, it appeared that controlling the dark powers inside him was appetizing work, plus he'd only eaten once in over a week. Kurt decided to venture into the outdated kitchen in hopes of finding something to eat. When he entered the kitchen, Kurt was surprised to see the three older women from earlier. Since it was nearly eight pm, Kurt assumed the women would've been asleep, but instead, the lively trio was wrapping peanut butter and jelly sandwiches in cellophane. Kurt cleared his throat and introduced himself, speaking loudly, not because of the women's age but because of the loud droning that came from the refrigerator in the corner.

"Excuse me, ladies, or should I call you sisters? I don't think we've met. I know earlier today there was a huge misunderstanding here that I would like to apologize for. My name is Kurt."

"If by misunderstanding, you mean almost slicing a teen's throat, but we knew you didn't have it in you."

Kurt extended his hand to each of the women.

"I'm Sister Mary Katherine, and this is my sister, Sister Mary Francis, and this is Sister Anna Marie." The woman in the middle of the trio said.

Kurt took a moment to find distinctive traits to tell the women apart, but it wasn't easy in the outdated kitchen's soft lighting. Sister Anna Marie looked like she had fallen asleep out in the sun for nearly 30 years. Her yellow blouse made her sun-kissed weathered skin glow. Age spots occupied her sun-battered face. It looked like life had been cruel to the five-foot woman. However, there was a level of familiarity in her eyes that caught Kurt's attention. The old nun smelled of perfume and cigarette smoke, her fingertips stained yellow from the nicotine. The other two women were practically identical in every way. Both were pale, standing next to Sister Anna Marie, super short and squatty. Even though they were no longer in a Catholic establishment, the two sisters still kept somewhat traditional outfits. Both sisters wore black skirts, white blouses, and thick, Velcro black shoes. Their black and white outfits made the squatty women look like aged penguins. The only difference between the two was that Mary Katherine's glasses had red frames while her sister's frames were blue. The glasses magnified the women's eyes, making them look like wrinkled grasshoppers with their large eyes, droopy cheeks, and bony appendages.

"What's so funny?" Sister Mary Katherine asked Kurt.

"Nothing," Kurt lied. "It's just hard to tell you two apart."

"I'm the younger, hotter one," Sister Mary Francis chimed in.

"She wishes," Sister Mary Katherine said. "We are identical in almost every way except our eye color."

Kurt leaned in and examined the two nuns. Sister Mary Katherine had eyes as blue as the sea. In comparison, her sister's eyes were green. There was also a tint of rebelliousness that flowed from both of the sister's eyes. Kurt also took that moment to examine Sister Anna Marie again. The sun-kissed nun leaned away as Kurt leaned forward, like a woman trying to avoid a kiss from an aggressive suitor.

"Her English isn't perfect," Sister Mary Katherine explained.

"She's visiting here from Peru. She wanted to see the American struggle, so she came here. She arrived a few months ago."

"Sister, this is Kurt!" Sister Mary Francis shouted at the Peruvian nun.

"Why are you yelling? I don't think she's deaf. Her English is just a tad off," Kurt said, smiling.

Sister Mary Katherine began laughing at her sister. Moments later, Sister Mary Francis joined in the laughter, followed by Sister Anna Marie. The three women were all laughing together. The image was almost too much for Kurt to bear; he also joined in. Kurt wondered if Sister Anna Marie even knew what was so funny. Exhausted from the day's adventures and feeling a tinge of anxiety approaching, Kurt stifled a fake yawn and prepared to excuse himself from the kitchen and head back downstairs to the storage room.

"Well, ladies, I think I'm going to turn in."

"We could fix you a room upstairs. It's probably better than that dank, dark storage room," Sister Mary Francis said to Kurt. "Then again, given the shape of this place, maybe not. Sometimes I miss the good old days when we provided help in a place that didn't look like it should be condemned. Don't get me wrong, I love helping people, but sometimes I wonder if we should even be in this building."

"I don't want to put anyone out. The cellar is fine with me," Kurt said, turning heading downstairs.

"Well, at least take something to eat," Sister Mary Katherine said, kindly handing Kurt a sandwich from the pile that was resting on the table in front of her.

Kurt graciously took the sandwich from the aged woman.

"Well, are you going to stand there, or are you going to say thank you?" Sister Mary Katherine asked, her hands resting on her hips.

"Thank you," Kurt said sheepishly.

"You're welcome," Sister Mary Katherine said, smiling at Kurt. "If you need anything, don't you hesitate to ask. I'm not sure what you're going through, young man, but it will make sense soon enough. It's always darkest before the dawn."

Kurt wasn't sure if it was the hunger approaching, anxiety, or emotional exhaustion that occupied his body, but everything felt as if it would be okay for a mere moment. Kurt placed his sandwich and drink down on the table and uncharacteristically bent down and hugged Mary Katherine. From around the table, Sister Mary Francis came to her sister's aid, only to be pulled into Kurt's embrace also. Kurt placed the two sisters on the ground and turned to hug Sister Anna Marie. To Kurt's surprise, the Peruvian nun was nowhere to be found.

"She's one of the fastest nuns in the world." Sister Mary Francis said jokingly. She fixed her attire that had twisted during the hug before continuing her one-woman show. "She still does triathlons', holds the heavyweight belt in boxing, and can pull a school bus with her teeth."

Kurt smiled; there was no doubt in his mind that Sister Mary Francis must have been a court jester in a former life. Kurt picked up his sandwich, bid the two sisters a good night, and made his way downstairs.

CHAPTER

Kurt devoured the sandwich that the sisters gave him in one bite. It wasn't long before sleep, the cousin of death overtook Kurt and invited the nightmares to invade his mind. After several hours of tossing and turning through countless horrors, Kurt awoke. Desperately not wanting to return to the realm of sleep, Kurt lay on the old cot staring at the moldy ceiling, trying to disregard the voices in his head.

"You should go back to sleep. We need our beauty rest. Besides, your dreams are so entertaining, and you know what they say. Dreams are the windows to the soul."

Determined to fight the urge to sleep, Kurt tried to occupy his mind, but all he could think about was Leah. Longing to see her again brought uncontrollable tears to Kurt's eyes. The feeling of heartache, loneliness, and desperation that Kurt felt was unbearable. What if scenarios played through Kurt's mind. If he weren't a pathetic loser and had told Leah how he felt, she would've known, and they wouldn't have been in the back alley. What if, instead of being scared, he had manned up and protected her? The world would no doubt be better if Leah were here, and he was the one who would've died. The spontaneous breakdown that Kurt was going through drained him emotionally, and he gravitated back to the realm of sleep.

Kurt's mind immediately banished him back into the dimly lit alley, where the three interlopers had destroyed his life. This nightmare was so realistic that the rain's downpour carried the scent of smoke from Dawn's. Kurt made his way down the alley, trying to escape the rain, but there was no cover. The metal awnings that had lined the alley were all melted from the intense fire. Wiping the rain from his eyes, Kurt noticed a figure standing at the alley's end. Kurt tried to call out, but he could not form any words. Kurt nervously brought his hands to his face, only to discover he had no mouth. Panic began to overtake Kurt as he fell backward in fear into several trash cans causing a loud commotion. The figure at the alley's dark end, hearing the crash, stepped into the light to investigate. Standing at the end of the alley in the downpour was Leah. She was dressed in a black dress and was holding a bouquet of dead black flowers. Kurt tried to pick himself off the ground, but his wet clothes weighed him down as he attempted to stand and approach Leah. Leah waved at Kurt as she began to run towards him. The rainfall, which had now become torrential, began to burn Kurt's skin. Kurt looked down at his exposed hands; they had started to blister and bleed. Carrying what felt like three hundred pounds of wet clothes, Kurt managed to stand and make his way towards Leah, but before he could reach her, the black dress she wore seemed to come alive. The dress began to swirl around Leah as if an unseen massive gust of wind propelled it. Leah tried to hold down the dress, but the more she struggled, the more the dress seemed to consume her. The bottom of the dress flew up and hit Leah in the face. Leah tried to pull the dress down, but the acidic rain seared the dress to Leah's skin. Leah let out a torturous scream. Kurt tried to reach out to Leah, but the acidic rain had melted Kurt's legs to the ground. He had no choice but to stand as the black dress liquefied over Leah's body. Kurt tried to turn away, but he couldn't break his gaze from the mutilation. As Kurt began to sob, a recognizable voice from his mind called out from the liquefied body that had once been Leah's.

"We can save her just as we can save you. Do not fear our power. We have been with you for your entire life, speaking to you, guiding you, protecting you. Soon we will be one. Only we can save you, and in return, you can save her. This nightmare is only the beginning for your friend. Leave this place while you can. Wake up!"

Kurt was jolted awake by screams coming from the upstairs of New Beginnings Church. Grateful that he was no longer dreaming, Kurt bolted from the storage room, up the stairs through the kitchen, past the banquet room, and up the soggy decaying stairs. The scene that awaited Kurt wasn't what he'd thought he'd see. Michelle was on a cot, similar to the one that Kurt had in the storage room. Michelle writhed on the urine-soaked bedsheets crying and screaming that she wanted to leave and go with Spider. Elias was trying to calm his goddaughter, but it seemed like his words were falling on deaf ears. Sister Mary Katherine and Sister Mary Francis hovered in the hallway in matching sleeping gowns like children watching their parents argue, trying not to be seen.

"Michelle, please calm down. You're going through withdrawal," Elias begged, trying to place a damp towel on Michelle's forehead.

"Fuck you! I don't want to be here. Where is Spider? You can't keep me here! Why the fuck are you old bats staring at me? "Michelle screamed at the sisters in the hall.

"That's the drugs talking child," Sister Mary Katherine said. "You know we care about you."

"Shut the fuck up, you old hag!" Michelle shrieked, breaking free from Elias and heading right at Sister Mary Katherine with surprising speed. Her drug-ravaged body looked sickly and erratic in its movements, and her eyes had a wild look to them, similar to that of a rabid animal. The elderly woman's face went pale; she didn't stand a chance of evading Michelle's attack. Kurt, sensing that the impact from a drug mad Michelle, would mortally injure the elderly nun and knock her down the decaying stairs. Kurt stepped from behind the sisters and intercepted Michelle's attack. Kurt caught and shoved Michelle forcefully, who fell back onto the floor with a loud thud.

"I'll kill you too, mother fucker!" Michelle screamed at the top of her lungs.

"Please forgive her. She knows not what she's saying," Sister Mary Katherine spoke. "The drugs have warped her mind.

"Go to hell, you know it all bitch. If I get my hands on you, you're going to be sorry."

Kurt looked down at Michelle; she was scratching her skin and shivering. Kurt was not an expert on drug withdrawal, but he was sure these were some of the symptoms. Michelle's eyes were dull; her cheeks were taught and frail. She looked like a walking skeleton. The oversized shirt and pants she now wore were three sizes too big. The front of the oversized t-shirt was drenched with sweat as if Michelle had just run a marathon, but the temperature in the room was rather cold. Michelle's new screams interrupted Kurt's observations of the unfortunate girl.

"The donation bin of New Beginnings Church has no clothes that fit anyone properly. I bet their sermons are one size fits none as well."

"You can't hold me here. I know my rights!"

"Oh, look, now she's an expert on due process. What law school do you think she attended while high on drugs?"

Consequently, Michelle's screams were beginning to give Kurt a headache. Kurt reached down and grabbed Michelle by the shoulders.

"Shut up!"

"Taking the more direct route we see."

Michelle stopped screaming instantly.

"Michelle, you don't need those drugs," Kurt said in a still voice. "You can function without them. Get your life back right now. I know you think your life sucks, but you're alive, which is more than I can say about my friends. I can't close my eyes for a few moments without reliving the nightmares. I would give my life to have everything back to normal, and here you are, crying about your next fix. You have a second chance to start living, so do it."

Michelle looked at Kurt blankly as if her mind was trying to absorb the words he had spoken. From the palms of his hands, Kurt felt warm energy began to radiate from them. Suddenly Michelle began to convulse savagely. Kurt tried again to remove his hands, but it was as if he was magnetically attached to Michelle. The harder Kurt tried to pull away, the tighter his hands clenched Michelle's bony shoulders. Michelle began to dry heave, and her eyes rolled back in her head. White fluid began to flow from the numerous puncture marks all over Michelle's arms.

"What are you doing to her?" Elias shouted at Kurt, undoubtedly alarmed at the strange turn of events.

"Don't take another step, padre!" Kurt replied sternly. He was not sure what was happening, but he continued to hold tight to Michelle. At that exact moment, it felt as if it was what he was supposed to be doing. Michelle's face began to retake shape, her cheeks began to fill, and her sunken eyes took on life again. Before everyone's eyes, Michelle's body began to transform from a drug addict to that of a young woman. The metamorphosis was instant; Michelle convulsed one last time and let out a rejuvenating scream before she passed out. Kurt gently released Michelle's unconscious body and laid her on the floor.

"It's a miracle," Sister Mary Francis and Sister Mary Katherine said in unison from their hiding spot in the hallway.

Elias knelt beside his niece, who was sound asleep and looked at Kurt in awe. Kurt nodded and turned to the two sisters, who had kneeled at his feet. "Sisters, please get up."

The sisters slowly rose, and Sister Mary Francis spoke. "Sister Ana Marie missed a miracle."

"Where is she?" Kurt asked. It was three in the morning. Where could an elderly Peruvian nun possibly go at this time of night?

"She tends to the homeless every other night down at the city's homeless shelter. They are understaffed and overused. In her home country of Peru, she runs a homeless shelter. She is a saint, but not like you," Sister Mary Katherine said.

"I'm no saint. I'm not sure what I am," Kurt said.

"You're a miracle. That's what you are," Sister Mary Katherine said again, hugging Kurt tightly.

Kurt swiftly peeled the elderly woman from around his waist and turned to address Elias when he saw something that made his heart slam to a stop in his chest. On Michelle's forearms were the same upside-down triangle tattoos with circle writing, the same ones that had also been on the leather-clad female's arms who attacked Kurt and Leah in the alley.

"Doubtful coincidence? Oh shit, that's the perfect name for our new band that we're putting together."

CHAPTER

Crime Log: Richmond Gazette

Today, our streets are much safer, thanks to the Richmond Police Department. Officers arrested eighty-three drug offenders yesterday in a massive multiunit narcotics operation. Police arrived at the condemned Richmond Metro Meat packaging plant yesterday afternoon after receiving a phone call from a concerned citizen reporting an assault in progress. When officers arrived, they found several suspects in need of immediate medical attention. However, an intense investigation is underway; nevertheless, police believe a turf war over drugs is most likely to blame for those who sustained injuries.

CHAPTER

T he rest of the night, Kurt found it impossible to sleep. There were so many thoughts running through his mind. Michelle had the same tattoos in the same spot as the woman from the alley. Could it be a coincidence? Of course, it could. Michelle didn't have any of the same features as the woman in the alley but, perhaps she knew her. Maybe they were best friends who decided to get the same tattoo, or maybe they were in the same sorority or social media group at some point and time.

"We could go upstairs and persuade her to talk. Everyone has a breaking point. Allow us to find hers."

Kurt remembered how much he enjoyed losing control earlier at the abandoned warehouse. The fear in the eyes of the guards was euphoric. Kurt tried to push the feelings from his mind to no avail. The dark power inside Kurt yearned to be free. It didn't want, nor could it be controlled, and this scared Kurt. At the warehouse yesterday, Kurt had wanted to inflict pain, and he did it without a care in the world. Kurt tried to recall the thought that triggered his dark change. It would come in handy when he found Sebastian and his handlers. However, he found it odd that there was no rage in his power when he was healing Michelle. It was as if peaceful, positive energy had flowed through him. This fact instantly made Kurt feel more relaxed about what changes were happening to him. Perhaps he was destined to heal and not destroy.

"To destroy is to heal. To live in peace, you must prepare for war."

Kurt must have fallen back asleep at some point because he awoke to the smell of homemade pancakes. The scent led Kurt to the old kitchen where Sister Ana Marie was singing a song in what Kurt presumed was Peruvian. Sister Ana Marie turned and saw Kurt and laughed somewhat nervously.

"Sorry," Kurt said. "Did I frighten you?"

Sister Ana Marie shrugged her shoulders and stared at Kurt with a blank look on her face."

"Right, you don't understand me."

Sister Ana Marie piled six pancakes on a plate and handed them to him. She pointed to the pancakes, which Kurt took as an invitation to eat. Kurt took a seat at the old kitchen table that fit perfectly with the old church's dumpster vibe. Looking at the thin pancakes in front of him, Kurt didn't know if there wasn't enough batter to make thicker pancakes or if this was a type of thin Peruvian breakfast wafer. Kurt's stomach didn't care why the pancakes were thin. Kurt poured enough syrup on his pancakes that his entire plate looked like a sticky mess and devoured the paper-thin pancakes. There was a newspaper on the table where Kurt was sitting. Not wanting to sit in awkward silence, Kurt found an article on the back crime page about yesterday's events at the abandoned warehouse. Kurt held his breath while he read. However, nowhere in the story was there a description of him or Elias. It would be hard to explain to the police why they were there.

"We are scared of no one. If the police ask questions, we will silence their insolent tongues. Guns and fear of arrest do not scare us. No human-made prison has ever been able to hold us."

Sighing, Kurt began thumbing through the morning paper. For some reason, an article in the Arts section caught his attention. "The

Codex Gigas exhibit starts today at the Virginia Museum of Fine Arts," Kurt read aloud.

"Codex Gigas?" Sister Ana Marie repeated.

"Yup," Kurt said, "Codex Gigas."

"Codex Gigas?" Sister Anna Marie repeated before breaking into her native dialect, talking extremely fast while waving her hands in the air. At that moment, Sister Mary Katherine and Sister Mary Francis entered the kitchen.

"Good morning," both Sisters said in unison, bowing to Kurt.

"What's up? Please don't bow to me. Can you understand what she's talking about?" Kurt asked, referring to Sister Anna Marie, who was still talking in what sounded like an untranslatable dialect.

"Sounds like she's talking in tongues," Sister Mary Francis joked. "Or perhaps she's been in the wine."

"What set her off? Maybe she's upset because she missed the miracle last night." Sister Mary Katherine presumed.

"No, I was reading an article about the Codex Gigas and," Kurt began before he was interrupted.

"Codex Gigas!" All three women said at once.

"Ok, what the hell is the Codex Gigas?" Kurt asked.

"It's known as the Devil's Bible," Sister Mary Katherine said, crossing the room and taking the newspaper from Kurt. "It says the rare book is here at the Virginia Museum of Fine Arts. We should go see it."

"I don't know," Sister Mary Francis said nervously, staring down at her wrinkled hands. "I'm not sure I want to see anything the devil created. I've seen enough evil in this world to last a lifetime."

"But it is a priceless artifact, regardless of who created it," replied her sister. "It's a once-in-a-lifetime event. Plus, I have a membership, and I can bring up to five people with me free of charge."

"This ancient artifact has a pass to a museum to see other ancient artifacts. Are we the only ones who see the irony in this? Is this considered a double entendre?"

"Codex Gigas?" Sister Anna Marie chimed in.

"If it will stop her from saying that, I say, what the hell," Kurt said, voicing his opinion before realizing he was in the presence of present and former nuns. "I mean heck."

Smiling, Sister Mary Katherine spoke. "Well, when we have completed the lunch service, we will go see the..."

"Codex Gigas!" Sister Anna Marie finished.

Kurt smiled. After all that he'd been through over the last few days, maybe a museum trip could be relaxing.

CHAPTER

Around ten a. m., the sisters began welcoming in the volunteers working in the soup kitchen. Once the sisters assigned the volunteers their positions for the day, an influx of people started to flow into the church's open doors. A glance around the room revealed to Kurt how diverse the crowd was. All races and ages were affected by the decline in the economy. The sisters had told him earlier that the number of people who came for food had tripled in the last few months. Kurt was pained to see that a decent percentage of the homeless were small children, being force-fed by their parents, undoubtedly trying to have their children eat as much as they could hold in their tiny stomachs'. If New Beginnings Church were to close its doors due to the building's condition, or the apparent lack of funds, Kurt could not help but wonder how many more people would be directly affected. Kurt excused himself, but not before apologizing to Trevor, the dish boy from the previous day. He found it shocking that Trevor was not angry at all. Being held hostage by Kurt for a few minutes had made Trevor instantly popular with the high school girls he volunteered with. Glued to his arm, presently was one of those high school girls. Trevor accepted Kurt's apology but told him not to worry about it. Trevor gave Kurt a wink that said it was all worth it as he led his new girlfriend into the kitchen.

"Now that kid knows what he's doing. You should see if he needs an intern."

Kurt made his way upstairs, searching for Pastor Elias to speak to him about what happened last night with Michelle. Kurt knocked and entered the room where Michelle was resting. Kurt was expecting to see Elias, but to Kurt's surprise, he wasn't there. Michelle was sleeping peacefully on her cot in the corner of the room. An empty single padded card chair rested against the wall. Elias's butt imprint was still fresh on the fabric of the chair. A beam of sunlight filtered through a set of dirty, torn blinds and shined down on Michelle.

"All we're missing is a few singing animals, and we'd have a new-age fairytale."

Kurt silently agreed with the obnoxious voices in his head. Michelle's face was healthier than it had been the day before, and she looked so peaceful lying there in her supersized t-shirt. From nowhere, anger consumed Kurt. It invaded his thoughts like a menacing tumor.

"She sleeps while Leah wilted away. Death took Leah from us. Michelle was returned to her family. She bears the same markings as the woman in the alley; you should punish her for her obvious involvement, regardless of the lack of proof."

Unconsciously Kurt approached Michelle's bed, his eyes turning black, with a purpose of imposing pain. Kurt was jolted back into reality by Elias's voice, which came from the hallway behind Kurt.

"Kurt, are you okay? Kurt, can you hear me?"

"Sorry, I guess I zoned out," Kurt lied, turning around to face the former priest, his eyes reverting to normal. "I'm still kind of woozy from last night."

"That's an understandable statement, young man. Never in all my years have I seen anything like what you did. You brought Michelle back from the brink. I am in your debt," Elias said, gazing at his goddaughter, who lay resting in bed.

"You don't owe me anything."

"Michelle is the one who owes us some answers."

Michelle began to stir from her bed. She called out for her parents and then for Spider. Elias instantly went to Michelle's bedside and tried to comfort her. After a few soothing words, Michelle drifted back to sleep.

"I'm sorry to be rude, but she's restless. Can we carry on our conversation later? I want to give Michelle my undivided attention."

"So do we."

"I understand, Padre. I'll go help the sisters with lunch while you stay with Michelle," Kurt said, heading back downstairs.

"Thank you, Kurt. Once Michelle is okay, I will help you figure out what happened to your friends."

"You most certainly will, or you will die trying."

CHAPTER

16

Kurt passed the time by helping the sister's plate food during the afternoon lunch service. After Kurt had served the last person, he made his way to some of the empty lunch tables and began wiping them down with a damp rag and a bottle of watered-down all-purpose cleaner. Kurt kept his head down, not wanting to stare at the hundred or so remaining patrons who were consuming the only meal they conceivably would have that day. Kurt glanced up only a few times to check the large clock that rested over the door of the dining room. Sister Mary Francis and Sister Mary Katherine smiled at Kurt awkwardly whenever their eyes crossed paths. Inside, Kurt snickered; it was like they were all bearing a deep dark secret. Sister Ana Marie made her rounds around the banquet room, unaware of the trio's unseen promise. Kurt observed Sister Anna Marie pretend to pull a quarter from behind the ear of a skinny child. Kurt saw the child smile in wonder. Sister Anna Marie gave the child the coin, who immediately turned and handed the coin to his mother. For a moment, Kurt thought sister Anna Marie was going to cry; instead, she rubbed the child's head and continued her rounds. A muffled conversation going on at one end of the many tables caught Kurt's attention. Since leaving Michelle's room, Kurt's senses were operating at an inhuman level.

"That's him; imagine him with a hood on."

"I think you are right. We should tell the police."

"What is he doing here? Do you think he is here for us?"

"Nah, let's get out of here. I don't want to find out."

Kurt saw two dirty, long-haired, scraggly white men in filthy denim jackets get up from a table and hastily leave, knocking over chairs as they exited.

"Hey!" Exclaimed one of the diners eating near the table, clearly displeased that his meal had been disturbed.

Kurt decided to pursue the two men. The last thing he needed was the police asking around about his involvement at a known drug house. Kurt exited New Beginnings Church through the kitchen, which emptied into a vacant, trash-filled parking lot. Kurt's eyes scanned the parking lot, looking for any sign of the men, but there was none. All life in the area was currently inside, appreciating a free meal.

"These fools are in fear of their lives. Fear is nature's steroid. These clowns have already crossed the street. Their drug-riddled bones move fast. Allow us to open your eyes truly."

Kurt gasped as immense pain radiated from his head and into his eyes. It felt as if someone had driven red hot blades into his brain. Stifling a scream, Kurt fell to one knee.

"Wow, would you chill out for a hot second? It's not like we're searing your optic nerve with hellfire. You'd think you would be more appreciative of the ability to see longer wavelengths than those of visible light, which signifies the presence of warm-blooded prey in 3 dimensions. Allow us to give you a quick tutorial. Just follow the trail of stench from these two, and forget about everything else. We are predators, they are our quarry, and we are hunting them. It's that simple. Nothing else matters."

The voices in Kurt's mind quieted his pounding head and calmed his rocketing heart. Kurt hesitantly stood up, opened his eyes, and began to follow the two men's fear scent. The usually unseen yellow aroma fluttered in the air like the tail of a kite showing Kurt where the two men had gone. Kurt quietly dashed through the parking lot and crossed the street into a narrow alley filled with automotive windshield boxes and carts filled with glass panes. Crouching behind a stack of containers were the two men. Kurt approached stealthily.

"We will say we saw him there from across the street. That way, we won't implicate ourselves," one of the men said smartly. "I'm sure we would get a reward from the police or maybe Spider. We could get high for months if Spider is impressed with us.

"Or we could go back and capture him and turn him in ourselves, and then our reward might double. We took down the guy who took down Spider. We would be legends."

"Dead legends tell no tales," Kurt said, stepping into view and advancing on the two men. Through vermillion eyes, Kurt saw the men's body temperature skyrocket. The yellow fear that led Kurt to the men began to roll off in waves. The two men's eyes grew wide as they prepared to run. The red-eyed man who stood before them was dangerous regardless of how kind he looked. They had seen firsthand the carnage he was capable of inflicting. They had thought yesterday that he was a boogie man or a hallucination brought on by all the drugs. When they saw him in the New Beginnings Church free lunch line, they concluded that he was real and not an unnamed nightmare.

"Calm down, guys. I have no problem with you," Kurt explained, raising his hands as he slowly closed the distance between him and the two men. "I was there for Spider's girlfriend, Michelle. She's the goddaughter of Pastor Elias; he runs the lunch kitchen that you two unfortunate souls frequent for a free meal. Even though I'm sure you could probably afford food if you kicked your drug habit, but who am I to judge?

"Stop talking to them. We are the predator, and they are our quarry. Kill them; spill their blood to quiet their mouths."

Kurt swore he could hear the men's elevating heartbeats. Their fear amused him. Kurt continued talking to the men, not to give them peace of mind but to feed his ravenous ego.

"Now, if you two fine citizens decide to go to the authorities, then this free kitchen would probably close down, and we can't have that. Now, this can go one of two ways," Kurt explained, his eyes continuing to blaze. "You two can leave and never come back, or I can kill you right here right now."

"Kill them; do not give them a choice in the matter."

The two men took the first option and ran past Kurt as fast as their legs would allow. Kurt smiled mischievously as the two men ran away, terrified for their lives. Kurt turned and prepared to follow the fear that still hung in the air back towards New Beginnings Church, but to his surprise, Sister Mary Francis was standing there with a look of shock and disappointment on her face.

"It's not what you think, Sister," Kurt began to explain, his eyes still glowing with corruption and malice.

"Forget this old hag, go after your game. Those men have no worth, and neither does their word. They will report on your whereabouts, and we must remain off the radar for now."

The elderly woman held up her hand and silenced Kurt instantly. "I do not want to hear your lies. I can't believe you fooled me so easily, fooled us all. I read the newspaper, and you seriously hurt several people yesterday. Elias said you merely walked in and convinced Michelle to leave with you. He will be scolded for his lies, trust me. I guess you are not the person I thought you were. You took pleasure out of tormenting those two men just now. I will pray for your soul Kurt. My sister and Sister Anna Marie sent me out here to retrieve you; they are ready for you to accompany them to the museum," Sister Mary Francis said as she turned away from Kurt and dejectedly made her way back to the church.

"Sister, you don't understand. I can't control it, whatever it is. "It just overtook me."

"If a man be under the influence of anger, his conduct will not be correct." Sister Mary Francis responded impassively before she made her way back to the church, leaving Kurt alone in the alley to think about what she had said to him.

"So are we going to chase after those two guys, or not?"

CHAPTER

S ister Mary Katherine, Sister Anna Marie, and Kurt stepped off the public metro bus in front of the Virginia Museum of Fine Arts. Sister Mary Francis did not accompany the others to the museum. She said that she didn't feel well, but Kurt knew better. Kurt felt horrible that she had to witness his evil influence, but maybe a trip to the museum would pacify his conscience or, at the most, distract it. Despite the cold bitter January air, the line for admission wrapped around the museum. People huddled together tightly as they waited for the once-in-a-lifetime exhibit to open. Kurt was surprised at the number of people who were in line. Kurt wondered how many people had called out from work and how many kids had played hooky from school. Kurt escorted the two women to the back of the line.

Across the street, a group of approximately eighty people stood along the sidewalk protesting. They had several makeshift posters and were shouting absurd and cruel things to those waiting in line. The protesters were members of an extremist religious group that had nothing to do with religion. Leading this group was a balding, overweight white man in a worn long-sleeved outdated grey shirt that said God is the answer. Kurt could tell that the leader had enough charisma to attract a small number of followers and enough psychological strength to mold his followers to believe in his radical views. He clutched a worn leather-clad bible in his right hand and a megaphone in his left. The balding man had on a pair of stonewashed jeans that he probably bought with the t-shirt 15 years ago. His clothes may have been outdated, but his hatred and resentment were current.

"All of you are going to burn in hell," the man yelled into the orange and white bullhorn he was holding. "You risk the wrath of God just to lay your eyes on a book written by the devil."

"Perhaps we should leave," Sister Mary Katherine said nervously, her voice shaking as she pulled her hooded parka tightly around her wrinkled face, trying to block the cold and the protestor's hatred.

"Don't let them intimidate you," Kurt said. "Besides, if Sister Anna Marie doesn't get to see that book, she's going to drive me crazy."

"Codex Gigas!" Sister Anna Marie said right on cue.

"See," Kurt said, smiling.

"Oh, no," Sister Mary Katherine said, glimpsing at the protestors who had turned their attention to an interracial couple with a small child.

"Beastiality is punishable by eternal damnation!" The balding ringleader screamed, his congregation cheering him. "Mixing of races is a sin!"

"Stay here," Kurt told the two elderly women. Leaving them in line and going to the aid of the couple.

"Finally, it is time for some action. Shall we annihilate these fools? Do you think they speak in tounges and put their hands in bags with poisonous snakes? Those hypocrites are so funny, not to mention tasty."

"Tell me where it says in that good book that you are holding, that yelling hateful and ignorant things at people that you disagree with is okay," Kurt called out to the vile ringleader as he crossed the street.

"Silence his heart, and his mouth will follow suit. We should destroy him, kill one to save hundreds. This situation is on the verge of getting out of hand. Do not humor this cow. Having a debate with an idiot makes you look just as stupid, if not more."

"You are one of the unjust. The words in this book are a blueprint to live by," the balding ring leader shouted, lifting his bible over his head. His protestors cheered their approval at his answer.

"A blueprint, huh what does it say about getting your ass kicked due to your racist rhetoric? I'm going to ask you and your backwoods friends to leave before this gets worse for you."

"Stop giving options. We need to make an example of one of these fools, and the rest will kneel at our feet. Kill this hate-filled idiot in front of his group. Tear his tongue out first to show his words have no power, and then rip out his heart to show how worthless his life truly is."

"Joke, all you want. We speak the truth that you're too dumb to understand. It is not your fault, honestly. It seems based on your complexion you're only half-intelligent."

"Silence his graceless heart, and his mouth will follow. This situation is on the verge of getting out of hand. If his servants see him verbally assault you, then they will gain confidence. His words give them power. Eliminate his words by eliminating his ability to breathe."

Kurt angrily grabbed the balding instigator by his throat and squeezed, instantly silencing him.

"Kill this hate-filled idiot. Squeeze his neck until his head pops."

The voices in Kurt's head were right. People like this spewed hate and faced no consequences. They intentionally targeted people and made their lives miserable. Today they thought it would be a typical protest but oh, how they were wrong.

"After we silence this detestable douche, we may as well feed on the rest of these shepherdless sheep."

From their spot in the line, Sister Mary Katherine and Sister Anna Marie made their way to stand by Kurt. The two sisters sensed the situation was on the verge of erupting.

"Kurt, please don't let this man's ignorance blind you. His words are his own, do not hurt him," Sister Mary Katherine pleaded. "It is his right to be wrong."

"Don't listen to her! We could devour this entire pile of pathetic frauds that stands before us in seconds."

Kurt relaxed his grip from around the man's throat, surprising the man and his protestors. The balding ringleader looked from Kurt to the two old women with him. Using his salesman rhetoric, the balding man turned to his congregation.

"The devil's book is powerful. It has corrupted this half negroid boy and has manipulated these two timeworn women. The book is persuasive, but our words give us strength. Shout out your beliefs, let your words consume these devil worshipers like acid."

From behind the balding agitator, the congregation began hurling insults at Kurt and the two older women. The balding maestro smiled maliciously at Kurt and shrugged his shoulders nonchalantly.

"We told you this would happen. Silence their tongues by removing his."

Kurt looked on in disbelief. The anger and hostility that came from the protestor's mouths flowed so smoothly. There was no way that this was a spur-of-the-moment thing. It was as if each member of the hate-filled congregation had a Rolodex of harmful phrases they had stored over the years. They released a tirade of insults and derogatory words at Kurt and the two sisters. Sister Mary Katherine gasped as she was called a heathen and unsanctified. Even though she didn't understand the words, Sister Anna Marie knew she was being verbally assaulted.

"Do it now, or watch how these words wreck these two old crones."

The dark consciousness in Kurt's mind was right. This man and his congregation needed to be taught a lesson. Just because they didn't think something was right didn't give them the right to hurt others. Kurt's thoughts began to darken with evil intentions as he stepped forward, his fist clenched. A police siren blared from across the street as one lone cruiser slowly crept by. Over the loudspeaker, a deep, authoritative voice called out to the congregation.

"You cannot block traffic. Either get on the sidewalk or move along. Minister MacDonaugh, we warned you to leave this place over an hour ago. If you do not leave in two minutes, we will arrest you. Leave, or everyone goes to jail."

Surprisingly the group quickly quieted their vicious attacks and began to disperse, not wanting to attract the police's attention, leaving the balding ringleader by himself.

"Today must be your lucky day, boy. I had something special for you and these old women. Maybe next time."

"You should run away as fast as you can before I tear your throat out," Kurt said gruffly, the rage inside him begging to be released. "Or beat you the death."

The man backed away, smirking, never taking his eyes off of Kurt. After putting several yards between him and Kurt, the balding man waved, turned, and joined his fleeing congregation.

"Go after him. He is probably going to get reinforcements and will attack after this exhibit is over."

Kurt began to pursue the fleeing man and his congregation when a small hand grabbed his forearm.

"Please, no fight," Sister Anna Marie said in broken English. "Let them go."

"Now she can talk? She's just full of surprises, isn't she? When are we going to get to devour someone?"

Kurt looked down, surprised, and took the two elderly women by the hands and led them back to their place in line. As Kurt passed other museum visitors, many of them nodded silent thank you's in his direction. Kurt and the two women huddled together in the cold air like employees on a smoke break, trying to remain warm.

After twenty minutes, the museum doors opened. From within the museum stepped a man who identified himself as the curator. The curator told the crowd that the museum was open and the next tour was ready to begin, and for everyone to follow him inside.

"Codex Gigas?" Sister Anna Marie said excitedly, like a child going to see a movie for the first time.

As Kurt and the sisters approached the museum entrance, Kurt couldn't shake the feeling they were being watched. Kurt scanned the street but saw nothing.

"If you had killed those protesters, you wouldn't have to worry about them right now. It would help if you listened to us. We are wise."

"Maybe next time," Kurt said as he entered the museum.

CHAPTER

Kurt was amazed at the size of The Virginia Museum Of Fine Arts. Handcrafted tan marble columns held up the seventy-five-foot tall ceilings. The museum floor was the same marble but was polished to the point that your reflection stared back at you when you looked down. The architecture of the museum itself could poignantly be considered as a modern-day interior masterpiece. The entryway walls were lined with bronze plaques commemorating donors who helped remodel and revitalize the museum. Kurt smirked as he read some of the names. There weren't many Jones, Smiths, or Bryants on the wall, but several Vanlandingham's, Miller-Hardt's, and Pelletier's. The lowest contribution on the wall of donors was seventy-five thousand dollars. Kurt wondered if Elias had spoken to some of these donors to see if they could help New Beginnings Church. It would be of a high probability that most of these donors would say no.

A museum volunteer handed Kurt a brochure summarizing the Codex Gigas and led him and the sisters to exhibit room A. The room was well lit and located in the section that held other medieval works of art. A magenta velvet tarp covered a glass case that three large security guards surrounded. Another guard stood by the entrance, where people continued to flow through. While they were waiting for the room to fill, Kurt browsed the other artwork in the room. An oil painting hung in the corner that caught his eye. It was a decapitated head, held over a large silver platter. The picture was titled Salome Receiving the Head of St. John the Baptist by Andrea Solario. Kurt wasn't an art major, but he thought that the image was kind of grotesque.

"We like it, and you could learn a lot from this picture. Torn off heads tell neither secrets nor lies."

The museum curator waited until the very last person had entered the room before he spoke. The curator was a skinny-looking man in a wrinkled beige discount store-bought suit that was slightly too big for him. The man fit the role as curator perfectly, pompous and a know it all. His smart eyes scanned the crowd as he beamed, deducing that he was the most art-savvy person in the room. Kurt envisioned the curator was a victim of bullying in high school; he had the look of a former nerd who liked to flaunt his intelligence now that it mattered.

"My name is Harold Wells, and it's my pleasure to introduce you people to the Codex Gigas. I will give you a moment to take it all in. I know some of you have never seen anything so beautiful," Harold Wells said as he pulled the velvet tarp off of the glass case.

Smuggled in phones and digital cameras began flashing in a frenzy. Harold Wells quickly covered the priceless work of art as security guards began confiscating the smuggled contraband. It took a few moments before all the electronics were taken or placed back in purses and bags. After a short lecture on respecting the rules, Harold Wells again uncovered the Codex Gigas. Kurt felt a strange force in the room that made the hair on the back of his neck stand up. Kurt became unsettled and had to tell himself that everything was okay. Glancing to his left, Kurt noticed that Sister Anna Marie's sun-kissed face was expressionless. She stared at the Codex as if in a trance.

"Are you okay?" Kurt whispered.

"Codex Gigas."

Sensing that he wasn't going to get a real answer from Sister Anna Marie, Kurt turned to Sister Mary Katherine.

"It's so horrible, isn't it, Kurt?" Sister Mary Katherine said, her face white with fear.

Kurt looked away from the sisters and looked back at the Codex Gigas. Kurt was surprised at the size of the legendary book. The Codex was about three feet tall and about two feet wide. The pages of the book were brown with age. The Codex Gigas was open to a page that had a large illustration of the devil on it. The devil's face was green with two red horns protruding from its head. The eerie smile that was on the devil's face made Kurt uncomfortable. The devil's eyes were mesmerizing.

"Don't stare at the eyes. Trust us. The eyes are the windows to the soul."

Kurt struggled to turn away from the enthralled eyes of the devil. Kurt wasn't sure how long he'd been held captive by the picture's gaze, but it was more than a few seconds. Harold Wells had begun his presentation about the Codex Gigas' history and was already speaking about the legendary book's contents.

"The Codex Gigas contains the Vulgate Bible and many historical documents, all written in Latin. The Codex is composed of 310 pages of parchment allegedly made from the skins of calves. Initially, the book contained 320 pages, though some subsequently have been removed for unknown reasons. The book also includes a medical dictionary, which is very advanced for its time. This book was written a long time ago before there were all those internet medical sites that everyone uses for self-diagnosis."

The crowd didn't let Harold Wells's dry comedy attempt dampen their excitement from seeing a once-in-a-lifetime piece of art. Most of the group completely tuned him out as he continued to drone on. Harold Wells lectured on for a few more minutes before he removed his glasses and addressed the crowd.

"Now, we have a few moments left before we need to usher in the next assortment of art lovers," Harold said pompously. "Let's take the time for a few questions."

Hands shot up from almost every person in the room, including Sister Mary Katherine. Kurt smiled at the sister's excitement.

"Do you believe in the legend that one person wrote this book in one night?" someone called from the crowd.

"Well," Harold Wells began rolling his eyes. "Scientifically, it would be impossible for one person to complete this book in one night. Maybe they did have help, but I doubt it was from the devil. In tests to recreate the work, it's estimated that it would take one person twenty-five to thirty years of nonstop writing." Wells finished smugly.

"I heard that based on the handwriting, it was written by one person. According to the internet, the original manuscript was kept in a climate-controlled storage room and isn't on display for the general public. How do we know this is the real Codex Gigas?" Someone called out from the back of the room, clearly irritating Harold Wells.

"You only know what I tell you, and I'm telling you that it's real." Harold Wells responded sharply. "It was decided that the Codex Gigas should be shared with the rest of the world."

It was apparent that Harold Wells was bothered. His I am in charge, patronizing demeanor had quickly changed to that of agitated and anxious know-it-all.

"One more question, and then we must complete this little get-together of ours," Harold said, scanning the crowd for one last question.

"Does the Codex contain incantations on how to bring someone back from the dead?" Kurt called out without raising his hand.

"Of course, you ask the one question that will draw attention to yourself. We're supposed to be low-key until the time is right."

"Young man, that's a unique question," Harold Wells said, taking off his glasses cleaning them again on his tie before putting them back on. "The missing ten pages of the Codex are said to contain incantations on how to recall a soul lost to death. These pages have been lost, so it is impossible to verify if it could be possible. Several powerful exorcism spells have been translated in this book by Latin scholars. Many believe that the pages of this book contain evil. I think it's just a book written a long time ago. Just because it's old doesn't make it magical. People put too much faith in books written when times were different," Harold Wells said pretentiously. "Ladies and gentleman, we are out of time. Can everyone please make their way to the exits, please?"

"He's a lying stupid moron. The book possesses more power than he knows. You can feel it too."

Kurt half smirked in agreement as he and the sisters made their way to the exit. Kurt turned and took one last look at the legendary book.

"I will be back later for a more private visit," Kurt whispered under his breath. "I've got some questions that need to be answered."

CHAPTER

On the southwestern corner of the museum grounds, a battered Sedan sat idling in front of an old restored Confederate Memorial Chapel. The Sedans driver hid the vehicle behind a sizeable rusted cannon sitting outside of the front walkway. From this spot, the car had a perfect viewpoint to observe the back half of the museum, where people who had seen The Codex Gigas would be exiting. A large man sat in the driver's seat. Beside him in the passenger seat sat his pet, Sebastian. The driver had removed the entire passenger seat and frame so the beast could occupy the space. In the rear seat was a pale woman in a black lace corset, red skirt, and slingback stilettoes. Sebastian was resting until Kurt exited the museum with two older women.

"Easy boy, not yet," the large man said, petting the now livid beast. "Master said no kill, only watch."

Sebastian whined pitifully in approval and laid down, his hackles still raised.

"I don't know why the Master doesn't just kill that asshole," the woman said from the back seat. "I have other things, or should I say people, that I could be doing right now."

"Master said no hurt. We go now," the large man said as he pulled the battered Sedan away from the museum.

From the back seat, the woman blew a kiss towards Kurt. "See you soon, lover boy," she called out seductively.

CHAPTER

It was easy for Kurt to sneak out of New Beginnings Church. Since growing up in the foster care system, Kurt was acquainted with creeping around noiselessly and unseen. Not wanting to wake his foster parents, Kurt had developed many techniques of getting around without making noise. Tonight, Kurt would use those same methods from his childhood to slip out into the night. Kurt slinked up the stairs leading from the storage room, taking them two at a time. Opening the door halfway that led to the kitchen, Kurt slipped through it silently. Not wanting to use the outsized creaky back door, Kurt unlocked a small window over the sink and soundlessly exited into the night. Kurt kept to the shadows and recalled the route the city bus took earlier. Twenty-two minutes later, Kurt was standing on the brick walkway outside the Virginia Museum of Fine Arts entrance.

Kurt had no idea how he was going to get in. At 11 pm, Kurt knew the doors were going to be locked. To Kurt's surprise, when he pulled on the glass door, it opened. Kurt immediately knew something was wrong. Instinctively Kurt's senses went into overdrive, his body tensed, and his eyes begin to radiate black. Kurt smelled a lot of blood; he looked up and noticed two crushed security cameras. Kurts heightened hearing picked up the sound of muffled screams coming from the area that held The Codex Gigas exhibit. Kurt sprinted towards the stairwell that led up to the exhibition; he stopped at the door where the bodies of three security guards lay on the floor. It took Kurt's eyes a minute to process the scene before him. The bodies of the security guards were old and shriveled. The men's bodies all had the same pose, their arms outstretched as if they were trying to fend off something before they died.

"Only one kind of monster could've done this," Kurt said as anger and excitement took over his body, the creature that hurt Leah was close.

Kurt knelt and picked up two of the slain guard's collapsible batons and entered the hallway that led to the room that housed the Codex. Keeping to the shadows, Kurt quickly ducked behind a large marble column. Moving in a serpentine pattern from column to column Kurt quietly crossed the hallway and stopped at the exhibit room entrance. From his hiding spot, Kurt heard someone ask for the code to unlock the case that housed the Gigas. Kurt heard Harold Wells beg for his life. Harold said he did not have the code. Kurt couldn't help but grin. How the mighty had fallen, 12 hours earlier, Harold Wells knew it all, and now he was sobbing like a baby. Kurt decided it was time to act; whiny baby or not, Harold Wells didn't deserve the same fate as the security guards. Kurt grabbed an oak bench that was a part of the décor in the hallway and hurled it into the room that housed the Codex Gigas. The oak bench slammed into the adjacent wall with a loud crash. Wood splintered like shrapnel, and Kurt could hear the silver vases and teapots housed in the room behind the Gigas crashing to the floor. Kurt looked down at his hands in disbelief. He had thrown the bench hard enough to crash halfway through the wall that joined the two rooms with his magnified strength.

Using the oak bench as a diversion, Kurt entered the room that housed The Codex Gigas and raced towards Harold Wells. Kurt grabbed the crying curator by his collar and flung him out of the exhibit room into the hallway to safety. Now that the curator was safe, Kurt turned his attention to the thieves in the room. There in front of him stood the four monsters from the alley of Dawn's. The large man, the leather biker broad, the skeleton-like man, and the beast Sebastian.

"What in hell?" The large man said in broken English, his eyes scanning Kurt. A small smile crept over his face once he recognized the person standing in front of him. "You!"

"Me," Kurt said, staring down the behemoth in front of him.

Kurt noticed that the beast Sebastian was trying to circle behind him from the corner of his eye. Nature documentaries had been Kurt's entertainment as a child, and he instantly recognized that the beast was trying to flank him. Kurt reached for the batons that he borrowed from the fallen security guards. The creature hunched on its hindquarters and charged.

"I've got something for you," Kurt screamed as he turned and raced towards Sebastian, his eyes growing blacker.

"Bash him to death, teach Fido some obedience."

The beast charged at Kurt; the moonlight coming in through the windows illuminated every powerful muscle that lay under the coat of drab razor fur. The creature closed the distance between him and Kurt and lunged. Kurt was ready, and when the beast was midair, Kurt unsheathed the collapsible steel batons. A split second before Sebastian was about to land, Kurt placed both rods together and swung them like a baseball bat. The beast let out a pathetic cry as the batons found his jaw. The force of the baton hurled the creature back into the wall, landing on top of a great wooden chest that had been a part of the European art exhibit. Kurt wasted no time as he straddled the stunned beast and introduced the batons to the creatures muscle lined torso. Each impact caused the beast to squeal in pain.

"Do not stop! Use our strength to separate his bones from his body!"

"Get off of Sebastian!" The large man screamed, charging towards Kurt, hoping to rescue his pet.

"Moloch no!" Shouted the pale, wrinkled, skinny man who Kurt now assumed was in charge.

Moloch grabbed Kurt in a bear hug and pulled him off Sebastian, who now had several broken ribs and internal bleeding from being hit like a piñata that refused to surrender candy. Kurt slammed his head back, striking Moloch in the face. The behemoth of a man dropped Kurt and grabbed his mouth. The large man spit out several teeth onto the floor. Kurt smiled savagely and kicked Moloch in the knee with the heel of his boot. Kurt heard the man's knee shatter as he screamed in absolute pain.

"Yes, the sounds of pain are like music to us. We demand more. Play us a symphony."

"Shut up!" Kurt screamed to the voices in his head and the screaming big man. "This ends now."

Kurt raised the baton over his head, preparing to paint the exhibit room walls with Moloch's brain matter.

"No, please don't kill me!" Harold Wells screamed, causing Kurt to turn away from Moloch. In the exhibit room entrance stood the leather-clad woman holding a dagger to the know-it-all curator's throat. The blade itself was small and silver with intricate details on the hilt. The woman undoubtedly stole it from another one of the exhibits.

"Please don't kill me, don't let her kill me," Harold Wells begged Kurt.

"Kill him. I don't care," Kurt said, his eyes blazing as he turned back towards Moloch. To Kurt's surprise, the large man was standing upright, his knee perfectly fine. Moloch grabbed Kurt and punched him in the stomach, causing Kurt to double over. Moloch slammed his barrel-sized elbow on the back of Kurt's neck. Kurt slumped to the ground, dropping the batons. Moloch lifted a dazed Kurt with ease and slung him into the wall in the adjoining room some thirty feet away. Kurt slammed into the wall, every bone in Kurt's body rattled.

"Cilia, why don't you give Mr. Wells here a parting gift," the Slender pale man called out from underneath his velvet hooded robe.

"My pleasure Master," Cilia said, jamming the dagger into Harold

Wells' chest. Harold Wells let out a painful gasp and tried to take a few steps before he fell face down on the museum tile, blood beginning to flow from his chest. The dagger, even though a relic, had been sharp enough to cut through flesh. The thick, dark blood was filling into the grout of the marble tile.

"You can either follow us, or you can save this man's worthless life. The choice is yours," The Master explained to Kurt.

Moloch raced to the wall and ripped a large tapestry that depicted the Last Supper, and wrapped his injured pet in it with a surprising amount of care. He gingerly lifted the injured beast onto his shoulder before reaching down and tearing the case that housed The Codex Gigas out of the floor, like it was a weed in a garden. Carrying the two items, Moloch made his way back towards the windows in the museum. The museum alarm system, now operating on backup power, began to blare. Without pausing, Moloch put his foot through the glass, causing the entire window to shatter. Glass shards littered the floor and fell like rain, but the behemoth seemed unfazed as he walked right out of the museum and into the night. The Master exited the same way, his robe blowing behind him like a cape. Cilia left a bit more slowly. She took the time to blow a kiss at Kurt.

"We will meet again, no doubt," she called back to Kurt before she left, delighted at what had taken place.

"GET UP GO GET THEM! LET THEIR BLOOD FLOW FROM THEIR BODIES. WHAT ARE YOU WAITING FOR? DO NOT LET THEM LEAVE HERE ALIVE!"

Kurt had the urge to follow, but the moans coming from Harold Wells caused him to reconsider. Kurt got up and made his way to the injured curator, who lay face down in a puddle of his blood. Kurt carefully turned Harold Wells over. The antique knife protruded grotesquely from the curator's chest. Blood continued to swell from around the blade. Taking a deep breath, Kurt gripped the knife by its hilt and ripped it from the man's chest. A sickening crater was now present from the knife wound. Blood gushed freely from the hole and continued to pool on the museum's cool floor.

"I can help you; at least I think I can," Kurt said, placing his hand on the oozing cut. He could feel Harold's heartbeat weakening against the palm of his hand. Kurt knew he did not have much time; the man was losing a lot of blood. Kurt thought about the bleeding wound healing. From the palm of Kurt's hand that rested on the curator's chest, a warm white light energy flowed into the wound. Harold Wells let out a weak scream as he passed out. Blood soaked Harold Wells' shirt, but there was no gaping wound. Sirens in the distance alerted Kurt that time for admiring his handy work had passed. Kurt got up and used the same exit that Moloch and the others had used. Kurt felt terrible about leaving, but he wouldn't be able to explain what happened. And besides, who would believe him?

CHAPTER

"What the hell was I thinking?" Kurt said aloud to himself, punching the faded faux leather seat in front of him on the dimly lit city metro bus. "Why didn't I follow them?"

Kurt sat alone at the very back of the bus staring at his hands still stained with the museum curator's blood. Kurt looked up nervously and quickly put his hands into the pockets of his borrowed hooded sweatshirt. The bus was empty except for Kurt, an older black woman in a nurse's outfit who was nodding off to sleep, and a white-haired man dressed in a black suit. The white-haired man awkwardly looked away as soon as he noticed Kurt observing him. Kurt studied the man and his features. There was something that was out of place. The dark suit was tailored perfectly to the man's lean frame. The man's hair was completely white, almost transparent. The thinning strands covered several liver spots trying to hide in the mans receding hairline. The man looked back at Kurt and smiled insightfully.

"You didn't follow them because you had to save the curator's life. Tonight was not his night to die."

Kurt looked around the bus, slightly confused. He was sure that the man was talking to him, but he hoped that he was mistaken. Kurt already had enough problems in his life, and a clairvoyant caucasian on a city bus was another he didn't want or need. The elderly man got up from his seat and began walking towards Kurt. Even though the bus was maintaining its current 55 mph speeds through the city, the old man walked as if he was unmindful of the bus's motion.

"The choices we make shape us. If you spend all your time questioning the past, you will miss your future. Heed these words. You must make your choice," the strange man said. His piercing blue eyes felt like they were penetrating Kurt's soul. "I will explain more when we meet again."

The metro bus lurched to a quick stop, sending Kurt face-first into the faux leather seat in front of him. When Kurt looked up, he was surprised to see the white-haired man was gone. Kurt got up from his seat and made his way up the aisle, searching for the mysterious speaker. The bus driver opened the door and looked in his rearview mirror at Kurt.

"Sir, this is your stop."

"The old man, he must've fallen," Kurt called out, continuing looking under the seats of the bus, trying to find the white-haired man.

"Sir, there are only three people on this bus. Velma, myself, and you. There is no old man. Now, if you would kindly get off at your stop so I can continue on my way, it would be greatly appreciated."

Kurt looked around the bus, Velma was still asleep, and there were no other passengers anywhere. Kurt began to laugh as he pulled his hood over his head and exited the bus.

"Have a good night, sir," the bus driver said as he closed the door and pulled away from the curb, leaving Kurt alone with his thoughts.

"I think I'm going crazy," Kurt said aloud.

"You'll get no arguments from us."

CHAPTER

By the time Kurt arrived back at New Beginnings Church, he had just about pulled himself together. Using the snow piled up along the sidewalk, Kurt quickly cleaned the curator's blood from his stained hands. Kurt snuck around the back of New Beginnings Church to the kitchen. Kurt thought he would reenter the same way he exited, but someone had locked the window.

"You look like a guy who doesn't want anyone to know he was out," said a voice from behind him.

Kurt turned quickly, preparing to strike, but there was no danger facing him this time. Sitting in one of the chairs on the rear stoop was Michelle. She was wrapped in an old blue blanket, smoking a newly lit cigarette. The cigarette's orange ember pierced the darkness and eerily illuminated Michelle's newly life-filled face.

"Uh... Uh, I went out and left my key," Kurt lied.

"I doubt that. It looks like you left through a window, and you thought it would still be open. It would be best if you didn't lie. It isn't good for your soul. So I've been told," Michelle said, puffing casually on her cigarette.

"I am no angel; trust me," Kurt retorted, sitting down on the cold step across from Michelle.

"Well, you are something," Michelle whispered, putting out the cigarette and immediately lighting another. "I guess I should thank you, you know, for saving my life. Giving me a second chance, but I'll have you know I didn't ask for your help, so I don't owe you anything. I was doing fine by myself."

"Doing fine? Are you sure about that? You were living in an abandoned drug house with a guy who kept you high on drugs and treated you like shit. Oh yeah, let's not forget that you looked like that painting The Scream by Edward Munch. You were doing awesome. You should give self-help lessons since you were doing so well."

"Damn, why dont you tell her how you really feel. I mean, yeah, you're spitting straight facts right now but go easy. We need to get information from this cow before we slaughter it."

For a moment, there was no response from Michelle, only the crackling of cigarette paper burning.

"The scream," Michelle said between drags from her cigarette. "Damn, that is rough."

"See, we told you."

"Sorry," Kurt said.

"It is not your fault. I was such an idiot. I always fall for the bad boys. Spider was a distraction from me losing my family. And bam, before you knew it, I was addicted. It happened so fast it was like I was a prisoner in my own body until you set me free. Thank you for saving me."

Kurt nodded a silent you're welcome in the darkness. For the next ten minutes, the two newly acquainted strangers sat in silence until Michelle spoke.

"Can I ask you a question? What are you exactly?"

"I'm no one special. Never have been, never will be."

"At least you know who you are," Michelle replied seriously.

"Do I? I've lived in numerous foster homes but never felt like I belonged. I thought that was behind me, but now it's started all over again. Trying to fit in but knowing that you're different is a horrible way to feel. I want to be normal."

"It's not bad to be different," Michelle said. "My dad always said that to me."

"What happened to them?" Kurt asked. "Your parents."

Michelle was quiet for a moment, taking a long drag from her cigarette before she spoke. "I killed them. It was a rainy Friday night. I had gone out drinking with some friends, and I wasn't able to drive home. My so-called friends left me, they all piled in a taxi, but there was no room for me. So being the responsible young adult, I called my parents for a ride," Michelle said, lighting another cigarette. She stopped talking for a moment before she began again. "My parents were the best in the world. They both came to pick me up. They didn't judge me. They just loved me. Anyway, on the way home, here comes the irony. A drunk driver ran a red light and T-boned our minivan. My parents died instantly. Since I was passed out in the back seat, the paramedics said that I somehow avoided any injuries. So before you say it wasn't my fault, trust me, it was. I killed my parents. All the therapists and all the counselors all say the same thing. Michelle, you can't keep blaming yourself, well guess what, I do, and always will."

Kurt got up from his resting place on the porch step, walked to Michelle, and placed his hand on her shoulder. He wasn't sure what to say, so he went with what felt right. He began his own tragic story.

"I know the pain that you feel. You blame yourself, and what-ifs overtake your mind. You hear voices in your dreams. Your nightmares overshadow your sleep, and there are moments when you don't think that you can go on," Kurt said, swallowing the lump of grief in his throat before recollecting his own tragic story to Michelle. Kurt told Michelle every last detail. The New Year's party, the walk he and Leah took into the alley. The unprovoked attack resulting in Leah dying and everyone in Dawn's being murdered. Kurt even told Michelle what happened tonight at the museum. When Kurt was done, Michelle had almost smoked an entire pack of cigarettes.

"So what are you going to do next?" Michelle asked Kurt. "How are you going to find the three attackers?"

"The one called Cilia had the same tattoos on her arm as you," Kurt said. "I thought you were her when I first saw them on your arm. I had to resist the urge to rip off your arm."

"That is still an option."

"Tattoos? Michelle asked, pulling up her sleeves. "These aren't real tattoos," Michelle said, licking her finger, rubbing the tattoo, causing it to smudge. "I got this when Spider and I went to Oblivion."

"Oblivion?"

"The new techno-industrial Goth club that grand opened a few weeks back. There are several up and down the east coast. It's not a horrible business idea. A nightclub that also does tattoos. I was scared to get real ones, so I got these two Henna ones. Spider used to move a lot of product out of that place. Not to mention guns, prostitution, and whatever other illegal vices you can think of. The owner is a woman in her mid-thirties with black hair; she wears dark eyeliner and dresses in all black leather outfits. I think her name is Selena or something like that. She has an interesting reputation. They say she is a man-eater. Not like literally, you know, but they say she will sleep with a dozen men on some nights. I'm not one to judge, so girl, do your thing. Do you think she's the woman from the alley?"

"There is only one way to find out," Kurt said forcefully. "Where is this place located?" Kurt's eyes began to glow obsidian in the darkness.

"Easy man, chill," Michelle said, taken aback but not frightened by Kurt's ferocity. "It's nearly two a.m., which means the place is closing down. I doubt that you'll be able to stroll in there. I'm sure that Spider and his associates have made bail, and they won't be too happy to see you."

"I don't care who's happy and who isn't. I will destroy anyone who gets in my way," Kurt growled.

"You say that shit now, but we all know what you do when faced with a choice of fight or flight. Let us remind you that you had the

chance of spilling some blood tonight, but you stayed and treated that trembling whelp of a curator. Not that we're judging you or anything."

"You don't even know if Cilia and Selena are the same person. You can't just go in there and start destroying people." Michelle explained.

"I suppose you are right," Kurt admitted, his eyes diminishing back to normal."

"See, talk tough, and then you wimp out. Are we the only ones who see a pattern here?"

"We can go tonight," Michelle said.

"We?" "It's too dangerous. Elias won't allow it."

"Elias won't allow it," Michelle said, imitating Kurt. "What we're not going to do is think that Elias makes decisions for me. I'm almost twenty, technically an adult. He can't tell me where I can and can't go."

Kurt thought for a moment, Michelle was right. He wouldn't be able to stroll into Oblivion undetected. Especially after the ass-kicking, Kurt gave Spider and his crew. On the other hand, if the owner were Cilia, it would probably turn violent regardless. Kurt wouldn't be able to protect Michelle and take out Cilia.

"So, do we have a deal?" Michelle asked Kurt, interrupting his thoughts.

Kurt looked down at Michelle's extended hand and hesitantly shook it. He hoped he wasn't making a deal that would come back and haunt him.

"It's a deal but on one condition. You have to stop smoking. You smell like a smokestack."

"You drive a hard bargain," Michelle said, crushing the cigarette package in her hand. "Do we have a deal now?"

"Deal," Kurt said hesitantly.

"You should be careful who you trust. Only we truly know what's best for you.

CHAPTER

23

"This is Meredith Anderson reporting live from the Virginia Museum of Fine Arts, where last night the legendary Codex Gigas, as well as other pieces of priceless artwork, were stolen. According to an unnamed source from the Richmond Police Department, several security guards lost their lives during the robbery. The names of the security guards have yet to be released. There was one survivor, the curator of the museum Harold Wells. It is unknown if Harold Wells is a suspect in the robbery. However, he is being held for questioning. The museum's surveillance cameras did not catch any video of the robbers. The cameras in the entrance of the museum and the ones covering the Codex were destroyed. Detectives say that there were signs of a struggle. The thieves gained entry to the museum through the back entrance but exited by breaking out one of the priceless stained glass windows along the museum's side. Police are seeking to question a group of protestors who yesterday nearly incited a small riot. The protestors claimed the Codex Gigas was the work of the devil and needed to be destroyed. Museum officials have offered a seventy-five million dollar reward to anyone who could provide information leading to the Codex's return. Reporting live from the Virginia Museum of Fine Arts, I am Meredith Anderson with Channel 17 News."

CHAPTER

M oloch, Cilia, and the Master turned off the 6 A.M. news program and began to make plans.

"We have to be careful from this point on. The police are going to check every lead that comes across," Cilia said, her feet resting on the coffee table in her emptily decorated studio apartment on the second floor of club Oblivion.

"The police are no concern to me," The Master retorted as he kicked Cilia's feet off of the table.

Cilia shot him an annoyed look but said nothing to aggravate him further. The Master was already on edge, and there was a hint of manic energy in his voice when he continued.

"In a few days, this will be all over. We have the Codex, and I possess the missing pages. I am closer than I have been in centuries. With the missing pages, I will be able to return my soul from hell. We only need a few more innocent souls to exchange, and our plan will be complete. Soon I can be rid of this shell of a body, and we should act quickly. Sebastian doesn't seem very well."

In the corner of the room, Moloch knelt over his beloved pet.

Sebastian was in obvious pain; his stomach was bloated and making repulsive bubbling sounds. His skin was so stretched and bruised that it was possible to visibly make out tormented faces of the unfortunate souls caged within him. The beast was sluggish and unresponsive. The attack at the museum and all the pure souls he held in his stomach was causing Sebastian immense pain.

"It's okay, boy," Moloch said to his companion. "Master, Sebastian sick."

"I don't care what ales him, as long as he can regurgitate the souls that rest inside him is all I'm concerned about," The Master said as he glanced at the window and sighed dejectedly at the approaching sunrise.

The Master removed the scarlet hood, exposing his face to the rising sun. The left side of The Master's face drooped like a deflated balloon; his left eye bulged from the socket and sagged towards the floor. The left side of his face contained no bone at all. It had decayed over time. The Master reached into his robe and pulled out a small bronze orb. He placed the small sphere in his mouth and pushed it to the left with his tongue. The Master gasped in pain as the bronze orb began to grow and take the missing bone's shape in his decrepit face. The Master took several deep breaths trying to combat the pain surging through his ancient body. After a few moments, he reached back into his robe and pulled out a small black bag. He opened the bag and began applying makeup to his pale face. Once his disguise was near completion, The Master took a gold amulet shaped like an hourglass from the same black bag and made his way over to Sebastian and knelt in front of him. The Master placed the amulet in front of the wounded beast. Sebastian sniffed the charm and then began to breathe into it. From Sebastian's mouth, a mist flowed into the amulet. The amulet turned from gold to jade once the beast was done breathing into it. The Master stood up and placed the charm around his neck, and the transformation was instantaneous. The Master now looked hundreds of years younger. The Master removed his red robe and donned his disguise for the day.

"I need to be getting back. I can't wait until I no longer need to pretend to be something that I am not," The Master said disgustedly. "I will take the Codex Gigas with me. Where I'm going will be the last place anyone would look for it."

The Master lifted the large book with surprising strength, threw it over his bony shoulder, and headed for the door. Before he stepped out, the Master turned and addressed his cohorts. "You two will be rewarded for your loyalty," The Master said, closing the door behind him.

"Ancient Asshole," Moloch said, rubbing Sebastian's head, who whimpered in agreement.

CHAPTER

25

K urt found it hard to catch up on any sleep. He tossed and turned on his worn-out cot for hours. The butterflies in his stomach grew restless, waiting for the night to come. Since Kurt couldn't sleep due to the uneasiness, he decided to see if the sisters needed any help in the kitchen. Kurt got dressed in a simple pair of donated black jeans, a blue t-shirt, and a grey hooded sweatshirt. Surprisingly all these items fit Kurt perfectly. When Kurt entered the kitchen, Sister Mary Katherine and Sister Anna Marie were peeling potatoes over a large metal pan. Sister Mary Francis was not in the kitchen. Kurt wondered where the nun could be. Kurt hoped she wasn't still upset about what she had seen in the alley yesterday after lunch. Suddenly the door to the kitchen opened, and Sister Mary Francis scampered in. The cold morning wind slammed the kitchen door closed with extraordinary force, causing everyone in the kitchen to jump. Sister Mary Francis locked the door and began unzipping her jacket.

"Don't stop talking because I'm here," Sister Mary Francis said, flexing her shoulder.

"We weren't talking. I just got up," Kurt explained, sensing the former nun was still disappointed in him. "Are you ok? What's wrong with your shoulder? Would you like me to take a look at it?" Kurt asked, taking a step towards the elderly nun.

Sister Mary Francis quickly stepped away from Kurt fearfully and went and stood behind her sister.

"I am an old woman. The pain I carry with me reminds me that I am alive, and I wouldn't trade it for anything."

"Ok," Kurt said, holding both his hands up, surrendering. "I just wanted to help."

"I didn't ask for your help. Besides, I don't know if I could afford your help."

"She is lucky that we don't remove her disrespectful tongue."

"That makes absolutely no sense whatsoever. What's your problem?" Kurt asked.

"You're my problem. I saw what you truly were yesterday. You're an imposter, a charlatan," Sister Mary Francis began.

"Ok, children," Sister Mary Katherine said from behind the metal pan of potatoes. "We don't want to do this in front of Sister Anna Marie. Why don't we step outside and discuss this?"

Sister Mary Katherine excused herself and left Sister Anna Marie peeling potatoes while she ushered Kurt and her sister outside. The cold morning air cut right through the older women like a knife. Both women had on thick jackets that they had both wrapped tightly around their aged bodies, while Kurt wore a thin long-sleeved sweatshirt and a pair of jeans, yet the cold air had no effect on him.

"Damn, it's colder than a witch's tit out here."

Kurt couldn't help but smile.

"Is there something funny?" Sister Mary Francis demanded.

"Oh, I'm sorry, I didn't know I needed your permission to smile."

"Children!" Sister Mary Katherine shouted.

"Sorry," both Kurt and Sister Mary Francis said in unison.

"Ok, let's discuss the issues that are at hand," Sister MaryKatherine said, addressing Kurt. "My sister and I know what you did to free Michelle from the drug house. We know that you severely injured some of the guards. My sister tells me yesterday that she saw you possessed with evil. She says your eyes were red. We don't know what tricks you are up to; however, we think it's best if you leave."

"Tell her you were crying, or you were drunk. Why explain yourself at all? Tell them they are lucky to even be in our presence. They should bow at our feet. They should worship us!"

Kurt was taken aback by the brute honesty from the two nuns. They believed Kurt was evil, and that was all they needed to know. Kurt did not argue, the sisters lived here, and if they didn't want Kurt there, he had no choice but to leave. Besides, if there was one thing that Kurt was used to, it was being asked to leave a home. Even as an adult, he was unwanted.

"The nerve of those two prehistoric dinosaurs. We don't need their hospitality anyway. Soon they will be occupying two small plots somewhere. They don't have many sunrises left in them. We could make today their last if you want."

"If that's how you feel, then I will leave," Kurt said, shrugging his shoulders. "This place is your home. Thank you for letting me stay."

The two women exchanged puzzled looks. "That's it?" Sister Mary Francis asked Kurt. "No screaming at us on how we should bow before you and tremble at your awesome power."

"Wait for it. It's coming, you ancient old hag."

"Nope."

"Again, you fail to listen to us, and again we are disappointed but not surprised."

"Maybe he's not entirely evil," Sister Mary Francis said, looking at her sister. "Any man who performs miracles as he did cannot be a servant of hell."

"What? This was your idea. You were the one who was sure that he was sent here to ruin everything," Sister Mary Katherine said defensively.

"You've said it yourself, I'm known for jumping to conclusions, and occasionally I let my emotions get the best of me. I have seen the error of my ways," Sister Mary Francis said apologetically to her sister as she prepared to escort Kurt back inside and out of the cold.

"Wait! This conversation is not done." Sister Mary Katherine said sternly.

Both Kurt and Sister Mary Francis stopped in their tracks and turned and faced Sister Mary Katherine, her arms crossed over her chest. It was evident that there was more lecturing to do.

"Kurt, you are more than welcome to stay here. Unlike my sister, I am not so easy to forget evil deeds. I am not sure what evil lives inside of you, but I know it exists. It lives in the heart of even the most humble servants. I have the utmost confidence that you can control it. I fear that if this evil is left unchecked, it could grow to consume you. We will not allow you to go down a path of destruction and maliciousness," Sister Mary Katherine said, her eyes searching Kurt's, making him feel uneasy.

Kurt closed his eyes and bowed his head, breaking the sister's transfixing gaze. Kurt tried his best to sound genuine as he spoke. "You're right. I will try my hardest to control myself," Kurt said, giving Sister Mary Katherine his most docile look. "I promise."

"Wow, you are a natural at this. We will enslave humanity in no time."

Sister Mary Katherine smiled at Kurt warmly and walked over and hugged him. "It won't be easy, but rest assured that you will have the support of everyone here, including Sister Anna Marie, Sister Mary Francis, and myself."

"Us too, we will always be with you. Were like a bad case of the crabs, you'll never get rid of us. We're like the gift that keeps on giving."

"Thank you," Kurt said, returning the sister's hug and silently cursing the voices in his head.

Kurt followed the two elderly women back inside, thankful the conversation was over. Lying had always made Kurt feel uncomfortable. It wasn't the lying but the fact that he was so horrible at it. The two sisters took off their jackets and immediately went back to helping Sister Anna Marie peel potatoes for today's lunch special. Kurt decided to make himself useful. Kurt picked up a broom and swept the floor, and emptied the trash. While Kurt busied himself, the three sisters began to talk. Their conversations ranged from politics to the state of the world today. Kurt was surprised at the views the women took on specific topics. Considering their Catholic background, Kurt was somewhat surprised to hear Sister Mary Francis and Mary Katherine supported particular issues. These former nuns were not afraid to go against society and its popular beliefs. From time to time, Sister Anna Marie would nod and say something in some inaudible language. Kurt decided to ask the nun a question to see how many languages she knew.

"So, Sister Anna Marie, tell me a little about yourself."

The tanned nun continued to peel potatoes, ignoring or not understanding Kurt's question.

"Sister," Kurt repeated, this time raising his voice a little.

"She doesn't speak English. She's not deaf," Sister Mary Francis said from behind the mountain of potatoes.

"She speaks English," Kurt said. "At least a little anyway."

Sister Mary Katherine explained to her twin sister what transpired at the museum yesterday. Leaving out not a single detail, the long-winded nun informed her sister of the protestors and the near riot. Ten minutes into the story, Sister Mary Katherine finally got to the part that Sister Anna Marie spoke briefly yesterday in English.

"Good for her. She pretends that she can't speak English, which probably saves her from talking to idiots. I'm going to try it the next time someone asks me something stupid," Sister Mary Francis said jokingly. "Maybe she's just shy, don't push her. She will talk when she's ready."

Kurt agreed with Sister Mary Francis and decided to drop the subject. Maybe Sister Anna Marie didn't have anything to say. Kurt went back to sweeping, and the nuns went back to peeling potatoes in silence. In no time, the pile of potatoes dwindled until they were nearly gone.

"Is there anything else you need help with?" Kurt asked the nuns, noticing that they had begun to clean up the potato peelings. "Is that all we're serving today?"

The elderly nuns continued to clean up their pile of potato peelings, not answering Kurt. Kurt waited a moment and then repeated his question with the same result. None of the nuns even looked at him. Sister Mary Francis began to cackle, instantly joined by her sister.

"That was fun. I can see why Sister Anna Marie pretends she can't speak English. You should see your face," Sister Mary Francis said between giggles. "We're also going to serve lobster bisque and scallops to go along with our potato soup."

Kurt shook his head at the laughing nuns. The tension that occupied the kitchen earlier that morning had faded away and Kurt begin to laugh also. Kurt picked up the pan of potatoes and took them to the antique oven. Kurt and the sisters continued cleaning when Elias stormed into the kitchen with Michelle in tow. In the former priest's hand, he held a newspaper that he had rolled up like a weapon.

"Looks like someone in this room is in trouble. Our money is on you. And by our money, we mean your money. Since we know that you're poor, there's no money even to put on you."

Elias crossed the kitchen and headed directly to Kurt. "Where were you last night?" He demanded as he jammed a finger into Kurt's chest. His face was tinted scarlet with anger, and his breath was coming in gasps.

"Good morning to you too," Kurt said, trying to ignore the finger in his chest.

"Don't be snide with me, young man," Elias replied hotly, his face growing redder by the second. "Answer the question! Where were you last night?"

"Judging by the newspaper that you are brandishing like a machete, you know where I was last night."

"Yeah, you tell him. Or tell him to piss off."

"Elias, what's the problem?" Sister Mary Katherine asked.

Not taking his glare off of Kurt, Elias unrolled the newspaper back into its proper form and began to read. "Last night, The Virginia Museum of Fine Arts was the scene of a unique museum theft. The Legendary Codex Gigas was stolen during a daring art heist. Sources say that the thieves made off with the priceless relic by blowing a hole through the wall. Several museum security guards lost their lives during the theft. The only survivor of the heist was museum curator Harold Wells. At the moment, police will not say if Mr. Wells is a person of interest. As Mr. Wells was led away by police, he gave a vague description of a man he said was involved in the heist. Mr. Wells says the man is a 5'11 black male, one hundred and eighty pounds, with black hair and eyes as black as the night sky. During the robbery, Mr. Wells stated that he received a fatal stab wound but that the man healed him. Authorities say Mr. Wells was covered in blood, all belonging to him, but had no wounds. Police have no leads. A reward is expected to be offered for any information in regards to the Codex in the upcoming days."

After Elias finished reading, the kitchen grew quiet until Kurt spoke. "You think that was me? Come on, that description is so vague it could be anyone." Kurt joked. "It's not what you think. The people who attacked me in the alley with Leah were there. They were stealing the Codex Gigas. I tried to stop them, but they nearly killed the curator. So I let them go to save his life," Kurt explained.

"You had no right going there. You put this church and everyone in this room in extreme danger," Elias said, raising his voice.

"This guy must be crazy, how he dare lecture us on where we can and can't go. You better handle this; let him know who's in control."

"Don't tell me what rights I have!" Kurt said, struggling to control his anger. "You had no problem sending me in to retrieve Michelle. Well, now I want answers about what happened to my friends. I am an adult, and I will do what I need to do to avenge my friends. I didn't steal the Codex, and if you don't believe me, then you can go to hell. From this moment, anyone who stands in my way will be sorry!" Kurt exclaimed as he slammed his fist into the kitchen table, his eyes turning black.

The old wobbly kitchen table exploded under Kurt's fist. Pieces of wood flew in all directions. The fear that now filled the kitchen excited Kurt. Sister Anna Marie's heartbeat seemed to skip a few beats as she cowered behind Sister Mary Katherine. Elias placed Michelle behind him and took a boxer's stance, his fist raised, preparing for a confrontation.

"Not bad. Now let's teach this fallen priest a lesson about fighting. He doesn't stand a chance against us."

Kurt was prepared to listen to the voices in his head when a gently placed hand on his arm jolted him back into the moment. Sister Mary Francis's bony hand was ice cold, but her gaze was fiery as she calmly spoke to Kurt.

"You promised that you would try to control the evil that engulfs your soul. Please calm down. Elias meant you no harm."

"Don't listen to her. She doesn't know what she's talking about. Let's kick his pathetic ass."

"I'm sorry, sister. You are right," Kurt said calmly, taking a deep breath to calm himself."

"Son of a bitch."

Kurt's eyes returned to normal, and the mood in the room did the same. Kurt bent over and began picking up the table he destroyed.

"I'll buy you a new table," Kurt said.

"With what? Your good looks? And if that's the case, we will never have another table," Sister Mary Francis joked.

The old sister was trying to put everyone at ease, and it was working. Everyone in the room began to relax. Michelle grabbed a broom and began to sweep up wood chips. The older women all pitched in by holding the dustpan and placed the debris into the trash can. After the damage had been cleaned up, Elias pulled Kurt aside and spoke to him."

"Kurt, I am sorry. I should have listened to Michelle. She told me not to accuse you until I had the entire story, but my anger blinded me. I am not perfect. I believe you young people say my bad."

"No worries," Kurt said respectively. "We will pretend like this never happened."

"We never forget."

"You said the three from the alley were at the museum last night. Do you think they are following you?"

"I have no idea, but now I know a little bit more about them. The large man is called Moloch, the woman is called Cilia, Sebastian is the soul-eating beast, and the old wrinkled ring leader is known as

The Master. I'm not sure what they want with the Codex, but I may have a lead. I know where one of them maybe later. Michelle and I are going to......," Kurt started.

"Going to what?" Elias asked.

Michelle, who had been listening from across the room, came over to explain her and Kurt's plan of infiltrating club Oblivion to see if Cilia was, in fact, the club's owner. The idea was immediately met with criticism and objections from everyone, even Sister Anna Marie, who understood the tones from everyone else in the room.

"I cannot tell you what to do. I can only advise you to be careful. Now, if you'll excuse us, we must begin preparations for lunch today," Elias said, leaving the kitchen unable to suppress his irritation. The three elder women apprehensively following in his footsteps.

"See, I told you he wouldn't say no," Michelle said to Kurt when they were alone in the kitchen.

"*Trust no one.*"

"I don't," Kurt said aloud.

"Don't what?" Michelle asked. Her question fell on deaf ears as if Kurt was a million miles away. Michelle left Kurt in the kitchen to be alone with his thoughts.

CHAPTER

26

M oloch answered the phone at club Oblivion on the second ring. "Hello, yes, Master, right away," Moloch said, hurrying to the base of the stairs. "Cilia Master on the phone!" Moloch screamed.

"Are you serious?" Cilia exclaimed from her bed as she reached over the body that she was dining on and picked up the phone. "Yes, Master. Are they coming here tonight? Are you sure? Yes, we will be ready. Do they suspect anything? I will call you when they are dead." Cilia hung up the phone and looked down at the sickly young man that occupied her platform bed. "Sorry, sweetie, where were we?" Cilia asked. "Oh yeah, I remember." Cilia climbed on top of the young man who once resembled a fit twenty-something. Cilia pressed her perfect naked body on his and began to kiss him. Each kiss, each touch, each moment of ecstasy stole priceless years of life from the man. As much as he wanted to stop, he could not. The young man couldn't get enough of Cilia. He had to have more. He had failed to realize that the thirty minutes of enjoyment had caused him to age seventy years. The once young man closed his eyes and willed himself to last a few more minutes.

"Is it good, baby?"

"The best, sweetie," Cilia said seductively, continuing to steal the young man's life.

The young man's heart stopped beating; his body had finally given in. Cilia looked down at the dead body in her bed in disgust. The once vibrant, muscular young man was nothing more than a shriveled husk. Cilia reached over the dead body and pulled a lever on her California King Size headboard. A trap door opened from the floor beside her bed, and Cilia disgustedly pushed the dead body down the trap door, where it joined countless more.

"Moloch, there's a gift for you in the basement. Please send me another lover," Cilia called out.

From downstairs, Moloch heard the trap door shut and shivered with excitement. Every time Cilia had a sexual liaison with someone, he got the leftovers. Nothing made him happier than dining on the flesh of the dead. After being with Cilia, the men surprisingly had a cinnamon-like aftertaste. Over the past two weeks, Cilia had been going through men like they were going out of style. And when she was done, Moloch devoured the evidence. Cilia's exotic beauty had been blinding men for centuries, and today's man was no exception. Moloch made his way to the waiting area where men lined up to lie with Cilia. Moloch opened the door and asked who's next. A small disturbance broke out as men punched and kicked each other to see who could satisfy Cilia's appetite. Several minutes of brutal fighting determined a winner. Moloch shook the young man's hand and led him upstairs to Cilia's room. He tried not to think about how he would dine on this man's bones later. As Moloch turned back and headed down to the basement to have his snack, he overheard the young man bragging to Cilia.

"Honey, Spider is going to give you the time of your life. You're going to remember this day."

Moloch shook his head in amusement. They always said something along those lines, not knowing that there has never been a man who could outlast Cilia.

"Man, stupid she won't remember," Moloch said aloud as he descended to the basement to dine.

CHAPTER

27

Today's lunch crowd seemed unusually large to Kurt. Kurt took several headcounts and came up with one hundred and sixty-two each time. There wasn't an empty seat anywhere in the moldy-smelling dining hall. What surprised Kurt even more, was as many people inside New Beginnings Church, an equal amount was waiting outside in the cold for their turn to come in and eat. Now that Kurt was a familiar face, several people smiled and waved at him. The extensive lunch crowd kept Kurt very busy. According to Sister Mary Francis, Kurt was assigned to trash duty since he was so young and energetic. Kurt's responsibility was to make his way through the tables and get rid of any trash that he saw. Kurt was so busy that he didn't have the opportunity to speak to Elias to ease his mind. After the lunch crowd finally dispersed, Kurt found himself surprisingly exhausted. Michelle, who had been on serving duty, made her way to Kurt as soon as the last patron had finally exited the serving room. Potato chunks covered the apron that she wore over her clothes.

"So, are you nervous?" Michelle asked.

"No, are you?"

"Hell yeah," Michelle said nervously.

"Me too," Kurt said. "If you don't want to go, let me know."

"I'm going; you saved my life, and I feel as if I owe you," Michelle replied, stifling a yawn. "We should try and get some sleep first."

"Agreed, when should we leave?"

"Oblivion opens when the sun sets, Cilia is usually there as soon as the place opens. I say we leave here around 8. Give the place a few hours to get going. That way, we can sneak in with the crowd."

"Okay."

"Alright, I'll see you tonight," Michelle said, heading upstairs to get some rest, leaving Kurt alone to finish cleaning up.

After the lunchroom was clean and reeked strongly of Pinesol, Kurt made his way down to the cold, damp storage room to get some sleep. Kurt had barely closed his eyes when the nightmares started. Kurt was in a pitch-black chamber of some sort. Even though the section was dark, Kurt knew he was not alone. Another presence inhabited this nightmare with him. From the shadows, Kurt could hear Leah's voice pleading to be released.

"Please let us go, please," Leah begged from within the darkness.

Kurt tried to follow Leah's voice, but he was lost and couldn't gain his bearings in the darkness.

"Please!" Leah screamed. "Kurt, please help me!"

"Leah!"

The dark presence that occupied the space with Kurt started to vocalize in a low, gruff accent." We can help you. If you want to save your friends, you will have to embrace us. We mean you no harm. Allow us to become one. Unleash your true powers, and you can end all this suffering."

"Help me!" Leah screamed again from the darkness, her voice sounding frantic.

"She doesn't have much time, Kurt. You can save her or allow her to suffer for eternity."

"Leah! Hang on, and I will save you!" Kurt screamed into the darkness. "I promise I will save you."

Kurt was suddenly ripped out of the darkness and jolted back to reality. Kurt awakened to Michelle's eyes, staring at him with a concerned look on her face.

"Are you okay? You were screaming. I didn't know if you were okay," Michelle said quietly.

"Yeah, I had a bad dream," Kurt said, sitting up. "Sorry I woke you, go get some sleep. I'll see you tonight."

"Sorry to break it to you, but it's 7:30. It's time to get ready."

Kurt looked at Michelle, stunned that he had been in the nightmare for over 5 hours. It had seemed like mere seconds. Michelle saw the concerned look on Kurt's face and asked him if everything was okay. Kurt lied and told her that all was fine, and he was just tired. Kurt stood up and stretched and faked a yawn to convince Michelle. After a few silent minutes, Kurt and Michelle made their way upstairs and slipped out into the night.

CHAPTER

28

"I thought you said this place opened when the sun went down," Kurt said from the passenger seat of New Beginnings Church's borrowed worn-out sedan. All the Club Oblivion lights were off, the large neon sign that hung over the two stainless steel black doors blared with ferocity. The neon light ricocheted off the doors and lit up the empty parking lot. The sidewalk that usually had hundreds of people waiting to get in was vacant. Even though all the lights were off, both Michelle and Kurt could hear the dull thud of techno music coming from inside.

"Relax; it must be a slow night," Michelle said.

"Or it's a trap."

"Did you call and tell them that we were coming?"

"Something doesn't feel right."

The green light of the digital clock that rested in the dash read 8:45 pm. The light cast an eerie tint throughout the entire vehicle.

"So let's go over this. I'm going to go in and say that I escaped from Elias and his church, and I'm looking for Cilia to see if she's heard from Spider. While I do that, you sneak in through the basement.

The club is the only business operating on this entire block, so no one will see you and call the police. You break in and see if you can get a glance of Cilia and if she is the lady from the alley. If she is, we can come back later tonight when everyone is gone and question her," Michelle explained to Kurt.

"No," Kurt said uneasily. The two-story brick building with its tinted windows made Kurt uncomfortable. "I will go in solo. You keep the car running. Something isn't right here."

"No way! I'm not staying!" Michelle exclaimed, opening the driver's door before Kurt could stop her. Michelle jumped out of the car and sprinted across the street towards club Oblivion, her skin illuminated by the sign's intense neon sign.

Kurt undid his seat belt and chased after Michelle. Kurt reached Michelle before she made it to the door of Oblivion. On the door of the club was a sign.

"Closed. Private party inside," Michelle read aloud.

"Okay, something is not right here," Kurt said, looking around uneasily.

"They have private parties here all the time," Michelle said. "Wait here." Michelle left Kurt standing outside as she slipped into the dark uncertainty.

"Michelle, wait!" Kurt called after Michelle to no avail.

"*This girl is either dumb or stupid. There is a difference. Trust no one, not even her.*"

"I know, I know," Kurt said as he too entered the club.

Inside club Oblivion, the smell of sweat, vape smoke, and liquor mixed in the air. The music that blasted over the speakers was screaming some inaudible verses. New age European techno beats drowned out most of the words. Strobe lights pulsated in unison to the beat of the music. Kurt shielded his eyes with his hand and followed the music's sound until it led him into a room that Kurt assumed was the dance floor. Fluorescent light engulfed this room. When Kurt's eyes adjusted to the light, he realized that he wasn't alone. In the room stood approximately fifty people, each one of them armed. In the middle of the room sat an older man with a spider tattoo on his neck. Next to him stood Cilia, who had Michelle in a chokehold and a knife at her throat.

"So glad you could make it handsome," Cilia said to Kurt.

Kurt felt his anger begin to boil. He had walked right into a trap like a fool. Kurt scanned the crowd, many of the faces he recognized from his encounter at the drug house. Few of the drug addicts were still sporting bruises and contusions from their earlier skirmish with Kurt. None looked happy to see him again.

"I see you know some of these people." Cilia said, noticing Kurt was scanning the room. "I think you've met Spider. He was so eager to prove that his manhood still worked after you assaulted him. I'm pleased to say that it did."

Kurt couldn't believe his eyes. Spider looked 150 years old. If it weren't for the tattoo on Spider's neck, Kurt would have thought Cilia was lying. The person introduced as Spider looked nothing like his former self. His skin hung off of him like a stretched-out t-shirt, and deep wrinkles lined nearly every surface of his skin. The man looked older than all of the elderly women combined at New Beginnings Church. It was utterly unbelievable.

"Did Sebastian get hold of him?" Kurt asked, trying to ascertain the cause of Spider's condition.

"No, baby. I did that to him," Cilia said flirtatiously, puckering her full lips in a seductive pout. "Don't you like it?"

"You did that? You may want to see a doctor because you've obviously got something."

"How do you think I've stayed so stunning after 300 years?" Cilia said, ignoring Kurt's insult.

"I'm guessing a daily dose of highly potent antibiotics."

Cilia loosened her grip around Michelle's neck and dropped her to the floor. Michelle fell to the dirty club floor and quietly scooted away until she had her back pressed against the bar. Cilia made her way over to where Kurt stood; she took long strides to exaggerate her hips' movement. It was a mesmerizing spectacle; even Kurt took notice of just how beautiful she was.

"You and I are the same. We are both beings of raw sexual

demonic energy. Beauty and the Beast," Cilia whispered into Kurt's ear, rubbing her body against his.

Kurt felt raw electricity travel through his entire body. It hurt, and yet at the same time, it felt so good. Cilia's voice was intoxicating, and her body was spellbinding. Kurt found himself committing Cilia's body to memory, every curve, and every bulge. Kurt wondered what Cilia looked like underneath her leather outfit. Kurt imagined Cilia's pale naked flesh illuminated by the fluorescent lights.

"I gave Moloch and his pet the night off so you and I could get better acquainted," Cilia whispered. "Let me get rid of this girl, and you and I can go upstairs. Why don't you let me give you a taste of what's to come."

Cilia placed her lips to Kurt's and parted his lips with her tongue. Cilia's tongue searched Kurt's mouth as if she were searching for a buried treasure. Reflexively Kurt's tongue responded with some parrying of his own.

"Trust no one! Unleash us, or all will be lost. We have guided and protected you from the day you were born, and it is time for you to embrace us. Free us now!"

Cilia pulled her mouth away from Kurt and smiled at her latest conquest. No man had ever been able to resist her. "I will be right back. Let me finish some business first," Cilia said, making her way back to Michelle, who was still crouched against the wall.

"Kurt, help me," Michelle pleaded, tears flooding up in her eyes.

Kurt tried to move but was unable to. Cilia's kiss had rendered him helpless; all he could do was watch as Cilia placed her hands around Michelle's throat.

"Unleash us now or watch another friend of yours parish at the hands of this succubus demon. Say the words to set us free, so we may finally embark on this magnificent partnership."

"Kurt, help me!" Michelle screamed as Cilia tightened her grip around her throat.

"Kurt's speechless right now, sweetie. He's so enchanted by me. I have that kind of effect on men. Some girls have it, and you don't," Cilia said mockingly.

"Free us now!"

"Kurt darling, is there anything you want to say to your friend before I snap her messy little neck?" Cilia called to Kurt.

Kurt looked at Michelle. Fear had overtaken her eyes; her whole body was trembling in terror.

"Honey, did you hear me?" Cilia called out again.

"Yes, I heard you," Kurt said, closing his eyes. "I summon you to come forth. You are set free."

CHAPTER

The fluorescent illuminated room went entirely dark even though all the lights remained operating, and a robust sulfuric smell overtook the dancefloor. Once the room recovered from the darkness, Michelle was standing beside Kurt, looking shocked but immensely pleased to be away from Cilia.

Cilia looked at Kurt, surprised. "How did you do that? If you were smart, you should have run away while the lights were out," Cilia said, apparently annoyed with Kurt now.

"The lights never went out," Kurt said gruffly, his eyes glowing black. "I never moved, and I'm not running from you or anyone else. You have underestimated me for the very last time. Anyone who wants to live, put down your weapons, and leave. I only want Cilia," Kurt said, his voice becoming deep and unnatural.

"Don't listen to him," Cilia barked. "We will kill them both."

"Last chance, drop your weapons and leave," Kurt said once again.

Even with the life or death decisions to be made, no one left despite the nervous glances exchanged.

"I guess you have your answer. You were going to rule this kingdom with me, but now you will die," Cilia said, bragging.

"It's their choice to die," Kurt said, turning his back to the crowd and Cilia. "Destroy them all. Leave only Cilia."

From within the fluorescent-lit room, a dark fog began to choke out the light. Light bulbs exploded as the shadowy mist reached them. The techno disco ball that hung from the ceiling became dull and fell to the floor with a thud. The air in the room became dense and humid as the fog choked the oxygen out. The thudding music became chopped and screwed before the darkness silenced it too. The dance floor that had been loud and well-lit was now tranquil and dark. From out of the blackness, a pair of red eyes appeared.

"What the fuck is that?" One of Cilia's crew said aloud.

Someone fired several shots at the pair of red eyes striking them. "Did I get em?"

The question was quickly answered by the reappearance of the pair of red eyes. Cilia and her crew watched in horror as the red eyes began to multiply and then started to move. Like predators in the jungle, they stalked their prey. Out of the blackness, the attacks began. Razor-sharp claws and teeth lashed out from the shadows tearing flesh and bone from bodies. The panicked screams were like a dinner bell to the creatures who hunted in the shadows. The smell of blood overtook the air as Cilia's crew was massacred. Several more gunshots rang out as people ran for their lives, but the creatures in the shadows were merciless. Men were picked off one by one, like a sadistic game of tag. Kurt watched his eyes as black as the shadows in the room. The creatures that were doing his bidding resembled rats. However, these rats were the size of small lion cubs. Razor black fur covered their bodies. Nine-inch razor-sharp teeth helped them tear through human flesh with ease. Six four-inch serrated talons adorned each of their paws, allowing for the amputation of limbs. The voices in Kurt's mind called to him.

"From the depths of hell, we have summoned these battle-tested creatures to aid us. Watch as they tear limb from limb and leave no one but the witch alive as you requested."

Kurt watched as men ran into each other, slipping on the blood spilled floor. The demonic creatures devouring anything they could get their hands on. The rats continued to multiply. The more they ate, the more they replicated themselves. The original twenty demonic creatures now numbered over one hundred. Kurt watched in amazement at the masterpiece he had created. Like a conductor in a great orchestra, Kurt pointed out hidden henchman and watched as his creations shredded them. From the corner of his eye, Kurt noticed Cilia trying to crawl away in the darkness. Kurt raised his arm, and several rats descended on her, concentrating their attack on her exposed midriff. Kurt watched as his demonic rodents chewed a hole in her stomach. Cilia began to scream in pain.

"Kurt, what's going on?" Michelle called out from behind Kurt. "Are you still here?"

Kurt felt an instant pang of regret. He had forgotten that Michelle was in the room. He had been so consumed with the destruction of Cilia and her crew Michelle had slipped his mind. Even though it was pitch black, Kurt knew that Michelle knew what was going on. Kurt turned and placed his hand on Michelle's arm.

"I'm right here. I'm sorry you had to hear all this. Let's get you into another room," Kurt said apologetically as he gently guided Michelle from the dark room into the lobby that was too pitch black. "Stay here, and I will be back in a little bit," Kurt said as he left Michelle on a leather couch by the front door.

When Kurt made his way back to the killing floor, nearly four hundred red eyes were waiting for him. Bones scattered the floor. They crunched as Kurt made his way through the stillness towards Cilia, who lay on the floor writhing in pain. Lying beside Cilia was the body of Spider, or what was left of him. Before the attack, Spider was a shell of himself. Cilia had drained him during their twenty-minute entanglement session. Now, all that remained was a skeleton with a small skin patch with the spider tattoo.

Kurt reached down and rolled Cilia over so he could speak to her. Inside Cilia's stomach, several miniature red-eyed mice were eating away at her intestines. With a flick of his wrist, the mice vacated

Cilia's stomach and joined the other red-eyed rodents awaiting their next command. Cilia was holding some of her intestines in her hand. Kurt could see the ghastly white flesh bulging out from her fingers as she desperately clung to them to keep them from continuing to spill from her body.

"Let me give you a hand," Kurt said. "You tell me what you know, and maybe I will heal you. I could make you as good as new. You will be devouring stupid young men in no time. Lie to me, and my companions will rip you apart, again and again. The choice is yours."

Cilia looked up at Kurt and into his dead black eyes and began to cry. Cilia had seen and done some horrible things in her life, and this was the first time in three hundred years that she'd ever been this scared. She had used her body to control men for centuries, and now it was torn apart.

"I will tell you anything that you want," Cilia sobbed.

"Good, that's the best choice you've made in this place all night," Kurt said, laughing.

CHAPTER

30

It didn't take Kurt long to acquire information out of Cilia. Kurt dragged Cilia by her hair into the kitchen behind the bar, listening to the voices in his head. The voices knew how to extract the delicate information Cilia was hiding. The stainless steel kitchen smelled heavily of bleach. Through his obsidian eyes, Kurt picked up large amounts of human blood on the stainless steel counter. Kurt smiled; ironically, the dance floor in the next room was submerged in blood, and no amount of bleach would help. Kurt found an old wooden chair and tied Cilia to it, and began interrogating her. Kurt asked Cilia a series of questions. At first, Cilia tried to play coy and not tell Kurt the information he wanted to hear, but the voices in Kurt's head easily persuaded him to punish Cilia when she lied. Using his shadowy rodent army, Kurt watched as the rats tore open Cilia's midsection with ease and began chewing on her intestines. When Kurt thought Cilia had had enough, he reached down and placed his hand over the wound and healed her. The experience was so intense that Cilia passed out several times, slobber running from her mouth. Deciding to take a break, Kurt ventured through the blood-soiled dance room and into the pitch-black hallway to check on Michelle, who was sitting on the floor, her head resting in her hands. When she heard Kurt, she quickly wiped her eyes and stood up.

"Kurt, are you okay?"

"Me, yeah, I'm fine," Kurt responded. "I just came to see how you were doing."

"I'm okay. How much longer do we have to stay here? The smell of blood is making me nauseous." Michelle asked.

"We should get back to the kitchen and finish our conversation with the witch."

"It won't be long now. We're almost finished with our questions for Cilia. Ten or fifteen more minutes, then we can leave."

"We're? Who else is in the kitchen with you?"

"What? No one, it was a slip of the tongue. It's been a crazy night, you know," Kurt said awkwardly.

"Quit wasting time with this stupid cow. Our talents are needed in the kitchen. The witch is awake!"

Kurt turned and headed back to the kitchen. To his surprise, Michelle followed. Kurt stopped in his tracks, causing Michelle to run into the back of him. "Where are you going? You should probably stay here," Kurt said, staring into Michelle's eyes.

"No way, you're not leaving me alone out here. Either I'm coming with you, or you can take me back to New Beginnings, but I am not staying in this damn hallway by myself!"

"Shall we dispatch of her? We have the means to."

Kurt looked at Michelle, and even in the darkness, he could tell she was dead serious. Kurt agreed that she could come, but she could not say anything during his interrogation of Cilia. As Kurt led Michelle to the kitchen, he told her to close her eyes when they passed through the dance floor so she didn't have to see the countless red eyes peering from the shadows. Kurt reentered the kitchen with Michelle in tow. Kurt led Michelle to the furthest end of the kitchen for safety reasons. Kurt then returned to Cilia, who was now awake, her head hanging with tears in her eyes.

"So, what does The Master want with the Codex Gigas?" Kurt asked, squatting down to Cilia's level.

Cilia raised her head and glared at Kurt. "I will tell you nothing else. I am not afraid of death. Kill me; I will only return to hell, where I am a legend. Maybe I'll drop by and see your pathetic father. Yes, I know who you are. I realized it once you summoned those rodents. I always thought you were a made-up story. A boy spawned from the divinity of heaven and the damnation of hell. I have seen the chaos that you called forth tonight. You are a chip off of the old block. Tell me something, do you cry at night for your tragic lost love like your pathetic father. Oh, did you not know any of that? Do you not know who or what you are? That's just beautiful. You've got a lot to learn about your past. Your father was such a waste of a dark, beautiful soul, even at his lowest point, I'm positive he'd be disappointed in you."

"Do not allow her insolence!"

Kurt impulsively punched Cilia in her stomach and instantly regretted that decision. Cilia gasped and doubled in pain for a brief moment before leaning her head back and beginning to laugh. Kurt knew that Cilia was trying to get into his head. Kurt was determined to finish obtaining his answers. Over the past hour, since Kurt had dragged Cilia back into the kitchen, Cilia had told Kurt many enthralling things. Kurt now knew that the souls that Sebastian had absorbed were collecting in his stomach. The Master needed some of the souls to sustain his life. Kurt also knew that Sebastian was a unique type of hellhound called a ravisher that The Master had obtained long ago. Moloch was a clay creation with a borrowed demon soul. The Master had created Moloch with some type of mystical shake and bake oven almost one hundred years ago. Cilia was a succubus demon who was also a practitioner of the dark arts. It was her talents that, too, kept The Master alive.

Cilia continued to taunt Kurt even through the excruciating pain that was taking residence in her body. She believed that if she angered Kurt enough, he would finish her. "Your father was a feared leader in hell's army. He controlled millions of dark souls. He'd make what you did tonight look like a walk in the park. Then he threw all that power away."

"Shut up!" Kurt screamed. The shadows in the room began to thicken and churn with excitement. "I don't care about my father. I want to know what The Master will do with those souls and why he needs the Codex Gigas. I will not ask you again," Kurt said as he wrapped his hands around Cilia's throat.

Cilia looked Kurt in the eyes and spit on him. "I told you that I was not going to tell you anything else, do to me what you want. I am not afraid of returning home to hell."

"Kill her right here and right now. Leave a message for The Master. Defile her body and tear her eyes out!"

"No, I'm not going to kill Cilia. I have something far worse in store for her," Kurt said as he removed his hands from her neck. Kurt closed his eyes and took three deep breaths as the thick shadows began to disperse. Kurt then opened his eyes and placed both his hands on the opposite sides of Cilia's head, and began to speak. "Your body will be set free; no longer will you feel the desire to be possessed by evil. Live again as you did before you met The Master."

Instantly as Kurt spoke those words, Cilia's whole body began to pulsate. It was as if someone had shot a million volts of electricity into her body. Through her violent seizures, Kurt could hear her teeth knocking against each other as she shook. It took all the strength that Kurt had not to let go, even though he felt as if he would pass out. Cilia began to scream in torment and anguish. A powerful surge of white energy exploded from her body. The blast was so strong it launched Kurt across the room where Michelle was standing, watching the events unfold. Kurt crashed into the wall and landed at Michelle's feet. Michelle bent down and checked on Kurt but kept her eyes on Cilia as she pulsed with energy. The energetic light soon stopped as quickly as it had started. Michelle helped Kurt off of the floor and allowed him to lean on her while he caught his breath.

From across the room, Cilia began to cough deeply. It sounded as if Cilia was going to cough up one of her lungs. Cilia's coughing fit lasted for a few moments. Kurt and Michelle exchanged puzzled looks as they made their way over to Cilia, whose face was now cherry red from coughing. Michelle reared back and slapped Cilia on her back, instantly clearing her airway. Kurt and Michelle watched as Cilia coughed up what looked like a black nine-inch slug. The black slug fell from Cilia's mouth but evaporated before it hit the floor.

"What have you done to me?" Cilia whimpered, tears forming in her eyes.

"I'm not sure; I was hoping that you would burst into flames and die an excruciating death. I think I made you a human again, or at least de-demonized you."

"Is that even a word de-demonized, or is it un-demonized?"

"Whatever the word, I don't think you're a demon anymore, which is probably bad for you considering the company you keep. What do you think will happen if you go and visit The Master? He probably won't take kindly to you telling me information. Who knows how The Master will act when he realizes one of his cronies no longer has demon blood coursing through her body. Maybe he will feed you to Sebastian."

Cilia began to sob; having her demon powers stripped from her was the worst thing that could've happened. The new heartbeat that now drummed between her lungs was the loudest sound in the room. The mere thought of having to live with the beating drum of mortality inside her made Cilia sick to her stomach. As Kurt's words began to sink in, Cilia began to laugh hysterically.

"This makes me more like The Master than you know. The Master will kill you. He will make you suffer, you and your new piece of ass. You didn't wait long to replace your true love from the alley, did you? Perhaps you didn't love her after all," Cilia said scornfully.

Kurt picked up a knife from the counter and approached Cilia. Cilia smiled, leaning her head back, longing for the death blow that Kurt was about to deliver and release her from the body that now-imprisoned her. Instead of striking a death blow to Cilia, Kurt cut her loose from the chair.

"You're free to go, but I will take this," Kurt said, removing a cell phone from Cilia's pocket. "I suggest you try to live a good life.

Like you said about my father, there's a special place in hell for fallen demons. Make something of yourself, or dont, I dont care. If I ever see you again, I will kill you on principle, plain and simple."

Cilia got up from her chair and drunkenly staggered towards the exit. Her body drained of its demonic power was awkward and bulky. She no longer paraded with lustful self-reliance. Cilia slammed her shin into the corner of a table and began to cry. She placed her hand on her leg and rubbed it. The newfound pain was something she would have to get used to again. Kurt smirked as Cilia exited into the world in human form.

"We should kill her now. You could bring her back from the dead, so we could kill her all over again, teach her not to screw with us."

"You're just going to let her go?" Michelle asked Kurt, echoing the thoughts of his mind.

"Yeah, she's no danger to anyone but herself now," Kurt said. "Besides, we have her cell phone, and we can see if The Master is on her friends and favorites list."

Kurt unlocked Cilia's phone and began going through the incoming calls, and noticed only one number had called her 24 times in two weeks.

"Dial it on speakerphone," Michelle said excitedly.

"Okay, here goes 555-4359," Kurt said, dialing the number. It took a moment for the phone to start dialing. The sound of the ringing phone was loud, but Kurt was thankful because it covered up the uneasy hammering of his heart. Kurt was about to hang up the phone when a familiar voice answered on the other end.

"New Beginnings Church. How can we be of service this evening?" Elias Manningham's voice said on the other end of the line.

CHAPTER

31

Kurt quickly pressed the end button severing the connection. Kurt glanced at Michelle; her facial expression was one of surprise.

"Did you dial the right number?" Michelle asked.

"Yeah, I dialed the right number," Kurt said, tossing the phone to Michelle. "I just hit redial."

Michelle caught the phone midair and too hit redial.

"Hello," Elias's voice said over the speakerphone.

Kurt held his index finger to his lips, telling Michelle not to respond.

"I don't know who this is, or if this is some sort of prank, but please do not call here again," Elias said rudely, slamming down the phone.

"Did you dial the right number?" Kurt asked scornfully.

"It doesn't make sense," Michelle said aloud to Kurt, who had started pacing back and forth trying to force himself to relax.

"It makes perfect sense to me. Former Father Elias hits me as he's coming from visiting his congressman on New Year's Eve. Coincidence, I doubt it. Maybe he ran into me after orchestrating the back alley attack. He uses me to spring you from Spider's clutches. He pretends that he cares about me, but he doesn't. He was furious that I was at the museum last night. He doesn't want me to put the church in danger, give me a break. The only danger for that church is that it should be condemned or torn down, for that matter. He hasn't even tried to help me find out what happened to Leah or how I can save her."

"*Finally, trust no one.*"

"You're right. Trust no one. Pastor Elias is involved in this. I should have listened to you all along."

"Listened to whom?" Michelle asked, giving Kurt a concerned look.

"What?"

"You said you should have listened to you all along. Who?"

Kurt thought about telling Michelle the truth, but he decided not to.

"*Trust no one.*"

"I didn't mean it like that," Kurt lied, hoping to satisfy Michelle.

"I can't believe Elias is involved," Michelle said, obviously content with Kurt's answer.

"I don't want to believe it either," Kurt said, continuing to lie. "But someone called that phone."

"Maybe it was one of the sisters."

Kurt gave Michelle a doubtful look. "Are you serious? Their bifocals and arthritic fingers make them prime suspects. They creep around at night and rob museums and make phone calls."

"Never mind," Michelle said dejectedly. "What about the people who come to the church for lunch. Maybe one of them called Cilia."

Kurt thought for a moment. He had encountered two of Spider's men at the soup kitchen. One of those men or someone else could have called from the church. "You could be on to something. Realistically it wouldn't be hard to sneak off and use the church's phone."

"So we can agree that Elias isn't in cahoots with Cilia and the others," Michelle said excitedly, her voice filled with false hope. "We should try and figure out who it is."

"Okay, but my number one suspect is Elias. No offense," Kurt said.

"None taken. You said your number one suspect, which means you agree there can be more."

Our money is on the fallen priest, and our money is your money. Why are you trying to make this foolish imp happy? The truth hurts.

Kurt gave Michelle a non-committal shrug. "We should get out of here, just in case someone comes by," Kurt said.

"What are we going to do with ......?" Michelle began, a lump forming in her throat as she thought of all the blood and bones she'd passed on her way to the kitchen.

"I haven't come up with a plan but, this building looks fairly old. I'm sure the electrical system is crap and liquor burns."

Sensing that Michelle was uneasy with the idea of arson, Kurt suggested she go and get the car. Kurt guided Michelle through the blood-soaked dance floor to the front door and watched as she ran across the deserted street and started up the old sedan. Kurt closed the door, began opening liquor bottles, and started pouring the alcohol all-around club Oblivion.

There is a quicker way. We are one now, and you have access to a plethora of new abilities. Allow us to show you.

Kurt closed his eyes and felt pressure began to flow through his body. Kurt's hands felt as if they were burning, but surprisingly he felt no pain. Kurt opened his eyes and saw his reflection in one of the shattered barroom mirrors. His eyes were black once again, and his hands blazed with scarlet energy. Kurt pointed his hands, and searing fire shot from his fingertips. The recoil was deafening as Oblivion erupted in flames. Within seconds the wooden building was engulfed. Concealed in the fire, Kurt saw infinite, tormented, burning faces. The faces were in pain, yet they could not call out for help. Their mouths had been sewn shut. The faces danced in the hellish heat, ravaging everything they came in contact with. Kurt watched in pleasure as his flames internally decimated Oblivion before he quickly exited the roaring inferno, sprinting to the car where Michelle was waiting.

"Holy crap! Faulty wiring and liquor did that?" Michelle asked, her eyes staring at the sizeable fire that overflowed from club Oblivion.

"Yup," Kurt lied. "Let's get out of here before someone sees us."

Michelle pulled away from the curb with more speed than she wanted, nearly hitting an oncoming car. The other vehicle had to swerve to avoid a head-on collision.

"Sorry," Michelle said to Kurt.

"I'm okay, but let's go before that car turns around and gets our plate."

A thunderous boom came from Oblivion, which caused both Michelle and Kurt to duck down in their seats. Glass and shrapnel rained down on the borrowed sedan.

"Alcohol and faulty electrical wire..." Michelle said with a mocking smile.

"What can I say?" Kurt said, shrugging his shoulders.

"Baptized by fire, and cleansed in the blood of the aggressors. All in all, not a bad night".

Kurt nodded in agreement as Michelle drove away from the black ash falling from the night sky like tainted snow.

CHAPTER

32

"Hurry up, Moloch," The Master said from the rear seat of a newly stolen Nissan that Moloch had recently acquired. "Cilia should have handled the boy and his bothersome playmate by now."

"Yes, Master," Moloch said, pushing the accelerator to the floor, slowly increasing the speed of the old car.

"You couldn't get anything better than this heap?" The Master asked, referring to the old jalopy.

From the passenger seat, Sebastian began to whimper.

"It's okay," Moloch said, leaning over to pet his friend, taking his eyes off of the road.

"Look out!" The Master shrieked from the back seat as a car pulled away from the curb and headed straight for the stolen Nissan.

Moloch hit the brakes and jerked the wheel, causing the car to swerve violently. The Master was tossed around in the back seat like a ragdoll. Sebastian whimpered as he slammed into the interior door panel. "Master, okay?" Moloch asked, bringing the old car to a screeching halt.

"I'm fine, you moron. Get a move on so we can see how well Cilia fared."

A powerful blast rang out from the darkness. Fire and red hot pieces of steel and brick shards rained down from the sky, slamming around the stolen Nissan. A structural beam landed in front of the car, creating a hole in the asphalt.

"What the hell was that?" The Master exclaimed, ducking behind the driver's seat. Once all the debris had stopped falling, The Master lifted his small head and peered over the seat. The view that greeted him took his breath away. A gigantic fireball stood where club Oblivion once stood. The burning flames danced out towards the heavens as if they were trying to set the night sky ablaze. The Master sank back in his seat and cursed under his breath. Oblivion was more than a bar. It had served as a rendezvous point for many of the Master's associates, not to mention most if not all of The Master's potions were in the club. The Master knew that if the club was gone, more than likely, Cilia was too. The Master closed his eyes and whispered a demonic incantation, searching for Cilia's demonic presence, but he found nothing. The Master felt a tear roll down his gristly cheek. Cilia had been The Master's most faithful associate. Secretly The Master yearned to feel Cilia's touch. Had it not been for his condition, The Master believed he could've taken Cilia to places she could have only dreamed. At his age and in his state being held together by dark magic and thread, sex could prove to be lethal. Even though they had never experienced each other's touch, the bond The Master and Cilia shared had been a special one. They were two lost souls who fed off others' life force, prisoners of their flesh, and dark urges. Nearing sirens in the distance, dragged The Master away from his thoughts.

"Let's go, Moloch," The Master said gloomily.

Sensing The Master's pain Sebastian slowly climbed over the seat and rested his head on The Master's fragile old lap. Sebastian looked up at The Master and licked his face with his large tongue, leaving a slick trail of spit down the side of The Master's face. The Master rubbed the beast behind the ears and smiled.

"It won't be long now, Sebastian. We will carry out our mission even if it's the last thing we do. The boy will pay with his life."

CHAPTER

33

Kurt and Michelle weren't ready to go back to New Beginnings Church and confront Elias. They both decided that they were hungry and searched for a place to grab a bite to eat. The green light that radiated from the dash now read 2:25 am. There were not a lot of places open at that hour. Michelle maneuvered the borrowed sedan into a Pancake Palace parking lot. The little greasy-spoon was faintly lit and nearly uninhabited except for several club-goers who too needed a 2:30 am meal. Kurt and Michelle exited the borrowed sedan and made their way into the fine dining establishment. Kurt opened the door, and the smell of bacon plunged him into famine mode. Kurt's stomach growled with approval. Michelle heard Kurt's stomach and smirked at him. Michelle led Kurt to a booth in the building's corner, far away from the five or so drunken club closers. It wasn't long before a waitress approached the table. The waitress was a slender white woman in her late fifties with large sleep-deprived circles under her eyes that no amount of makeup could cover. She had her overdyed blond hair pulled into a tight ponytail. Her white waitress outfit had a dingy tint from the grease that she also wore like perfume. Her name tag read Gina.

"What can I get for you?" Gina asked in a raspy, cigarette-smoking voice.

"Can we get a menu?" Michelle asked.

"We ain't got any."

"Oh," Michelle said, looking around the restaurant, noticing that the other group at the far end of the restaurant had menus.

"That's not my section," Gina said impatiently as she noticed Michelle's inquiring gaze.

"This is the problem with the world today; everyone has a chip on their shoulder. Why can't everyone be as easy going as us?"

Kurt looked at the agitated waitress and smiled. Gina smiled back, wiping her forehead with the back of her hand. Gina's pupils were dilated, and she was sweating profusely even though it wasn't hot. Kurt looked at Gina's arm; there was a bruise on her bicep shaped like a large hand. Kurt was sure there were probably more bruises on Gina's body. Gina saw Kurt looking at her arm and pulled her shirt sleeve down. Gina took out her notepad from the front of her apron and looked at Michelle.

"So, what do you want?" Gina asked again.

"For starters, I want you to lose the attitude," Michelle said.

"We will both take two coffees and two breakfast combos," Kurt said.

"See, he didn't need a menu," Gina replied bluntly, leaving the table.

"All I wanted was a menu," Michelle replied immaturely.

"Do you want to talk about what just happened?" Kurt asked.

"That horrible waitress, no, I'm fine," Michelle replied.

"No. Earlier than that," Kurt said, referring to Oblivion.

"You mean when Elias answered the phone?" Michelle answered, intentionally avoiding Kurt's real objective.

"No, about what you saw happen to Spider and his crew."

Michelle grew silent. The only noise she made was the noise of her sliding a half-empty salt shaker back and forth over the table.

"I'm sorry you had to see that. I'm not even sure what happened," Kurt began to explain before Michelle interrupted him.

"He was so old," Michelle said blankly.

"I'm sorry, what?" Kurt asked.

"Spider, he was so old. Like Cilia sucked his life from his body," Michelle said. "And then the room grew dark even though the lights were on. There were so many people screaming and so much blood."

"That was us. You're welcome for us saving your pathetic life twice in a week, but who's counting."

Kurt watched as Michelle relived the scenario, and he felt ashamed. Michelle's expression was one of dreadfulness and distress. Kurt reached across the table and took the salt shaker from Michelle's hand. "I'm sorry you had to see that," Kurt started.

"Don't be. You saved my life. As horrible as this may sound, I am alive because of whatever that was you did. I feel sorry for you. That you had to do that."

Kurt let go of the salt shaker and stared at Michelle over the table. "I saw you were in danger, and then there were these voices telling me what to do. I did what they said, and all hell broke loose. I couldn't just stand there and let someone else die, like Leah."

"You're welcome too."

"Stop blaming yourself," Michelle said to Kurt. "If you could have saved Leah, you would've. And you said it yourself; this isn't over. Besides, you defeated one of the people responsible for your loss. What do you think Cilia is going to do?"

"I don't know," Kurt said. "Who cares? I want The Master, Moloch, and Sebastian."

"Revenge is near as long as we're together. We will have our vengeance."

"So, what are you going to do about Elias?" Michelle asked.

"If he's lucky, we're only going to beat the truth out of him."

Kurt thought for a moment. Whatever answer he gave would have to be good enough to mislead Michelle. Kurt was sure that Pastor Elias had something to do with what happened to him back in the alley in Washington, DC. There was no way that all the events that led up to tonight were a coincidence. Kurt looked at Michelle over the table and lied. "You are probably right. It is doubtful that Elias is involved, but as you said, someone who comes to the kitchen is involved somehow. We are just going to have to find out who," Kurt said, hoping Michelle believed his lie.

Michelle smiled, relieved that Kurt no longer suspected her godfather. At that moment, Gina, their waitress, arrived with their food.

"Anything else?" Gina said, placing two coffees and combos on the table, spilling some on the table before walking away, not bothering to wait for their answer.

"What a hateful hag," Michelle said, taking a bite of her bacon. "She's just a horrible waitress, and not to mention an all-out bitch," Michelle said, her mouth full of food.

"This one is one judgmental heifer. Wasn't she a drug-induced skank when we met her a few days ago? Do not trust this one. She forgets where she comes from. A person who forgets where they've been has no idea where they're going."

Kurt nodded in agreement as he watched Michelle scarf down her food.

CHAPTER

34

"Stop here," The Master told Moloch. "We don't want anyone to see us.

Moloch pulled the scorched sedan to the curb. From where he parked a block away, he could see the New Beginnings Church. Moloch scuffed at the sight of the worn-down sanctuary. The falling gutters, sagging roof, and damaged outer structure were an eyesore. The overall deteriorated building was littered with trash and tagged with various amounts of graffiti. The windows that were not broken were covered with plywood. Empty beer cans and shopping carts filled with trash littered the parking lot. However, with all its superficial defects, the unseen power that radiated from inside was vast. A blinding light shone from within the church, causing Moloch to squint his eyes and turn away. Moloch wondered how The Master could stand such positive energy.

"Take care of the pet," The Master said to Moloch, referring to Sebastian. "It is almost time for us to complete our task."

"Where Moloch go? Cilia no more here," Moloch asked.

The Master groaned irritably, but Moloch and Sebastian were all he had left now. "Meet me here at 11:30 before the lunch crowd arrives, and I'll sneak you in. Hide Sebastian under your coat somehow. Until then, leave and don't blow it."

The Master opened the door and made his way towards New Beginnings Church. Moloch watched from the car as The Master looked back and nodded. Moloch put the stolen car in drive and pulled away from the curb. The Master watched until the two tail lights of the Nissan were distant. The Master pulled his disguise from a bag. With his wrinkled old hands, The Master applied the mud-like substance on his face and began to rub it in. The Master massaged the mud into place, molding his face into that of another. The Master completed his disguise by putting on his wig and a flower pattern nylon nightgown with satin embroidery at the bust. Several homeless community members were already waiting in line, huddled up, trying to stay warm as they waited for the soup kitchen to open even though it wouldn't open until noon. Those in line nodded and greeted The Master in his disguise as he approached.

"Hello, sister," someone from the line called out. "It's kind of late for you to be out, isn't it?"

The Master smiled and nodded, pulling a key from his pocket, he unlocked the door to New Beginnings Church and slipped inside.

CHAPTER

35

Richmond Gazette Front Page
Five Alarm Fire in Downtown District By Antony Cornicello.

L ast night, firefighters from three surrounding counties fought a raging fire in the downtown district. Firefighters were unable to restrain the fire, and all that remains of the once-popular club Oblivion is a mound of concrete and smoldering ashes. Fire crews responded to the call shortly before three a. m. but quickly realized that more units would be necessary. The Richmond Fire Department spokesperson said that he had never seen a fire burn that hot for so long. Several charred remains were removed from the building but have yet to be identified. Fire marshals speculate that the arsonist used an accelerant, causing the extended burning duration. Authorities are asking if anyone has any information to call the Richmond Authorities at 555-2157.

CHAPTER

36

L ike most nights, as of late, Kurt hardly slept. After tossing and turning for hours, Kurt was dressed and prepared for the day by six a. m. He made his way up the stairs from the storage area and carefully ascended the steps, trying not to make any noise, but to his surprise, when he entered the kitchen, the three elderly sisters seemed to be just getting in.

"Good morning Kurt!" Sister Mary Francis said with the other two older women in tow.

"Morning, ladies. You three are out early."

"The day doesn't wait for anyone." Sister Mary Katherine said, with Sister Anna Marie nodding in agreement.

"What's that smell?" Sister Mary Francis inquired, sniffing the air. "Smells like smoke," she continued sniffing Kurt and smiling as she handed him the newspaper.

"I don't smell anything," Kurt replied, taking the newspaper, doing his best to appear nonchalant. Kurt had taken multiple showers last night, but the stench of a demonic burning pyre was rather hard to cover up.

"Don't be ashamed of what we did last night. Some things must burn so others can grow in their place. Fire is the ultimate cleanser."

On the front page of the newspaper was an article describing the fire at Club Oblivion. Kurt quickly scanned the paper; his heart was thumping like a drum. Thankfully the authorities had no leads. Kurt peaked over the top of his newspaper to find all three women looking at him.

"If you thought Pastor Elias was angry from the museum spectacle, you know he is going to hit the ceiling when he reads this," Sister Mary Katherine began. "The article says they pulled remains from the club. Please tell us that you weren't the cause of their deaths."

"Technically, we were the cause, so if you say no, you wouldn't be lying. We gave you an option to save your friend, and you took it. Now in a court of law, we wouldn't advise you to lie. Who are we kidding? Yes, we would. Human laws dont apply to us."

"I wasn't the cause of their deaths," Kurt lied.

"Good boy."

"I knew it!" Sister Mary Katherine exclaimed. "That's why we bought every newspaper in a two-mile radius this morning," she finished with a mischievous grin.

Kurt glanced through the doorway, and to his disbelief, newspapers overflowed from the church sedan. Kurt turned to the sisters with a bewildered look. "How did you afford these?"

"We got your back," Sister Mary Francis said. "We stole them."

Kurt walked to the sisters and planted kisses on all of their wrinkled, leathery cheeks. Sister Anna Marie, who probably didn't even know what was going on, received a kiss as she tried to pull away.

"We don't want Elias getting angry, do we," Sister Mary Katherine said consciously.

"Why should we fear his emotions? Those very emotions are what make him weak. We fear no man that walks this earth or any that have walked it before him."

"I'll take responsibility for my actions."

"What actions?" Sister Mary Francis asked.

"For the fire," Kurt replied.

"What fire?" Sister Mary Katherine asked.

Kurt laughed as the two sisters surprisingly gave each other a high five. "What are we going to do with all of those papers," he asked, casting a look toward the station wagon.

"We figured you'd just burn them," Sister Mary Francis joked.

Kurt sighed; he had walked right into that one. "All jokes aside, what are you going to do with them?"

"What do you usually do with newspaper, Kurt? You read them," Sister Mary Francis replied slyly.

Kurt shook his head at the feisty nun. Excusing himself, Kurt made his way out of the kitchen and headed to find Elias Manningham to have a little talk about a specific late-night phone call.

CHAPTER

37

Kurt made his way through the run-down soup kitchen and went upstairs to the church's living quarters. As Kurt passed by, he noticed that Michelle's door was half-opened. Michelle was still sleeping. She was sprawled on top of the covers, still wearing her outfit and shoes from last night. Michelle rolled over and started talking in her sleep. Kurt quickly pressed himself to the wall outside of Michelle's door. He didn't want to explain why he was watching her sleep if she happened to wake.

"Spider," Michelle whispered in her sleep. "Spider, please let me go; I don't want to be here anymore."

Kurt immediately felt another stitch of guilt. Michelle had lost her parents, and last night she saw her boyfriend die at the hands of a succubus demon. Kurt wished he could erase the previous night from her memory.

"Pull yourself together. We have a job to do. Don't forget the voice on the other end of the line. The falsifier must be forced to confess his involvement."

Listening to his inner demons, Kurt made his way towards Elias's office and living quarters. Kurt knocked on the door and waited a minute before knocking again. After waiting a few moments and hearing no answer, Kurt tried the doorknob only to find it locked. Kurt's eyes began to darken; from his hand, a flash of blue flame quickly liquefied the doorknob. With a slight push on the warped door, Kurt entered the office.

"Pastor Elias, are you in here?" Kurt called out quickly, surveying the office space but did not see Elias. However, this did not stop Kurt from searching the room in his absence. Kurt wasn't sure what he was looking for, but he was confident he would know it when he saw it. Going through the Pastor's desk paperwork, Kurt uncovered a pile of unpaid bills and a defaulted loan letter from the bank. The desk drawers were utterly empty, but Kurt pulled them out and tossed them on the floor out of anger. Frustrated, Kurt exited the office and headed back downstairs. A rustling noise from the top of the stairs caused Kurt to turn around. Standing in a spot that had been vacant seconds ago was Elias Manningham, his arms crossed over his chest. Kurt's mind automatically referenced the night in the alley, how The Master, Moloch, Cilia, and Sebastian appeared out of thin air.

"Did you find what you were looking for?"

"I have now," Kurt responded. "We need to talk."

"Yes, we do," Elias said in return, glaring at Kurt.

Kurt followed Elias downstairs and outback behind New Beginnings church into an unpaved parking lot. The lot was fenced in and stretch the entire length of the neglected church. Elias walked into the church's garden, and Kurt followed. The plot itself was small and had the same battered look to it as the rest of the church. Many of the rows of vegetables were labeled. Kurt counted ten different vegetables that ranged from asparagus, garlic, spinach, pea's, and several types of winter lettuce and onions. Anyone who looked at the garden could tell that a lot of care and time had gone into it. The growing vegetables were all placed in neat uniform rows. There wasn't one single weed in the entire garden.

"We need a nice warm spurt. Maybe an early spring will bring some rain. It's good for the vegetables," Elias said, looking at the garden. "Also, good for fires, isn't it, Kurt?"

"What?"

"I said rain is good for putting out fires. Even ones at nightclubs."

"This fool thinks he's clever. Do not allow him to manipulate you."

Kurt smirked at the former priest. It was apparent that the sisters hadn't confiscated all the newspapers in town, despite their fantastic effort.

"I was up early this morning, and what did I see on TV? A story about a fire at a nightclub you inquired about. The club you thought was the hiding place of the woman you called Cilia. Anything you'd like to confess? Confession does wonders for one's soul."

"Confess the need to punch him in his smug face."

"Not really. I'm good," Kurt said with a casual shrug. "I don't think you're qualified to take confession considering you're no longer a priest."

"I see."

"You say you were up early?"

"I was."

"You were up pretty late too, weren't you?"

"I don't think so. I don't gallop around town, breaking into museums or committing arson."

"No, you don't set fires, but that's because you are more of a behind-the-scenes guy. You're the guy who gives the orders. Did you get any late phone calls last night?" Kurt asked, his anger beginning to boil to the surface.

Elias thought for a moment, then as if he remembered something important, he spoke. "There were two prank calls last night, someone playing a joke. When I answered the phone, no one said anything. Was that you?"

"Yup, it was me. I was calling the last number in Cilia's phone," Kurt said, slowly circling Elias, trampling on the vegetables in the garden.

"Why would Cilia have called the church?"

"You tell me," Kurt said, glaring, continuing to circle the now nervous pastor like a lion hunting its prey.

"Don't believe the lies this priest tells. We can not trust him. Force him to tell the truth. Time is not on our side."

"I don't know why you are looking at me like that. I am telling the truth."

"A lot of things don't add up for me. You just happened to be in Washington D. C the night I was attacked. You miraculously show up and bring me here. You throw a bitch fit when you found out that I encountered Moloch, Cilia, and Sebastian at the museum. Did I interrupt your plans? You are the voice on the other end of the line of Cilia's phone. I'm not entirely sure how, but you are involved. I'm tired of being jerked around. Your sly remark about me burning down club Oblivion wasn't a joke. Deep down, you are pissed that I burned down your hangout. Now that all the cards are on the table let's get all this out in the open. Come clean about your involvement."

"Words are futile. Make this liar bleed, and the truth shall flow from him freely."

"Listen son, I know I am not the easiest person in this world to get along with. I am not perfect; I try every day to correct my flaws. I swear that I am not involved in anything. I did receive a phone call, and yes, I was upset about the museum. I don't want to see you hurt. Also, I don't want any negative attention placed on this church. This place is all that I have, and many people depend on it. I will not allow anyone to dishonor this church. Regardless of the physical condition of this place, inside those walls, hope rings eternal. I answered the phone last night only because it was ringing. I was not expecting a call from anyone. So I'm going to ask you to relax, so we can discuss this without the situation escalating," Elias explained calmly to Kurt, whose eyes had begun to darken.

"Relax, relax, how dare you tell me to relax! I want answers, and I believe you have them," Kurt stopped circling and attacked.

Kurt grabbed Elias by the collar with both hands and began dragging the pastor through the garden. Elias barely had a moment to react. All those years spent training in the boxing ring had made him a decent fighter, but against someone Kurt's age, Elias knew he had to create distance so he could try and get away. Elias grabbed Kurt's right wrist with his left hand and yanked, throwing Kurt off balance. Kurt released the pastor's collar to steady himself. Sensing an opportunity, Elias shoved Kurt as hard as he could, placing as much distance between him and the black-eyed youth.

"Oh no he didn't! Tear out one of his lungs!"

Kurt was surprised at the quickness of the aging pastor. Regaining his balance, Kurt again approached Elias. Liquid black tears flowed down Kurt's face like mascara in the rain. The darkness that lived inside Kurt was yearning to be released. Deep down, Kurt knew he should calm down, but the angry voices were deafening in his head. Kurt's entire body felt like a pipe containing too much pressure, and he would burst at any second.

"I don't want to hurt you," Elias said again as he raised his fist and prepared to defend himself.

"Too late for that priest," Kurt sneered through his clenched teeth, his voice not his own. "You will never hurt anyone again."

Elias threw a quick jab that connected with Kurt's nose. Kurt's head snapped back violently, and blood began to trickle from his nose. Wasting no time, Elias threw a vicious left uppercut that caught Kurt in the chin. Elias grabbed his hand and winced in pain after the well-placed punch.

"Aren't you supposed to be kicking his ass?"

Kurt began to laugh. The blood that had trickled from his nose had stopped. He had already healed. "Is that all you got?" Kurt asked mockingly. "I figured you would put up more of a fight."

Angrily Kurt slammed his fist into the former priests' stomach. Elias doubled over in immense pain; it felt as if Kurt's hand was going to go through his body and out of his back. Kurt grabbed the priest by the back of his collar and flung him through the garden. Elias had been in many fights in his life, but today was the hardest he'd ever been hit. The pain was so excruciating he nearly lost consciousness as he bounced off the ground like a pebble skipping across a pond. Elias came to rest some thirty yards away from Kurt. The pastor tried to get up, but his body wouldn't respond. The pain in his stomach had now spread to his lower extremities.

"Kurt, please, I don't want to fight you."

"We're not fighting, well, at least you aren't," Kurt said, his voice growing more sinister. He had intended to merely frighten Elias into telling him what he needed to know, but the pastor had hit him. Not only had he hit him, but he also embarrassed him. Kurt's well intentions had quickly morphed into something more dangerous.

"*Unleash us. Let us finish the priest. Unleash us, unleash us.*"

"Shut up! I will unleash you when I'm damned good and ready!" Kurt screamed, grabbing his head with both of his hands, trying to silence his inner demons. "Now stop screaming at me!"

Confused, Elias tried to stand while Kurt was distracted, but again, his body refused to cooperate with him.

"Shall we try this again, padre?" Kurt asked, clearing the voices in his head. Leaning down, Kurt again grabbed Elias by his neck, lifting him like he weighed a mere few ounces. Elias closed his eyes and said a small prayer, bracing himself for the barrage of attacks that would most likely destroy him, but the onslaught never came. When his death didn't arrive, Elias opened his eyes and was grateful for what he saw. Standing behind Kurt was Michelle, and she was pointing a small pistol right at him. The sound of Michelle cocking the gun was one of the sweetest sounds Elias had ever heard.

CHAPTER

38

"Let him go," Michelle said, aiming the gun at Kurt. "Don't make me repeat myself."

Kurt turned and glared at Michelle, who was not alone. Both Sister Mary Katherine and Mary Francis stood behind Michelle. Both of them had iron skillets in their hands. Several volunteers from the soup kitchens early shift were with them also. In all, Kurt counted nine people. One gun, two skillets, and an array of other household weapons.

"Go back inside," Kurt said, turning his attention back to Elias, whose face was starting to redden as Kurt held him by his throat. "Let the adults talk, go inside and cry about Spider."

Michelle closed one eye and squeezed the trigger. The bullet struck Kurt in his left shoulder. Kurt dropped Elias on the cold ground and turned and looked at Michelle in disbelief. That disbelief soon turned to amusement as the bullet exited Kurt's shoulder and the wound began to heal.

"*Unleash us now!*"

"I told you I wasn't going to repeat myself," Michelle said coldly.

Kurt took an angry step towards Michelle and her companions. Michelle fired again. This time the bullet landed one inch from Kurt's foot.

"You missed. Your next shot better kill me, or I will kill you." Kurt said through clenched teeth, trying to reign in his temper and emotions.

"Kurt, I don't want to hurt you." Michelle began, her voice starting to quiver. "You saved my life, but I can't let you hurt the only family I have left. So please, I'm begging you, regain control of yourself, please. You lied to me. You told me you didn't think Elias was involved. You have been lying to us all, pretending that you care! Spider may not have been a good guy, but he did teach me how to shoot. My next shot will not miss, I promise.

"Her bullets won't hurt us, and you know that. Take that gun and put it in her mouth, and end her pathetic existence! Her life will amount to nothing anyway. She stands before a demon god and threatens you with a gun. Kill her; kill the whole damn lot of them! We need nothing from any of them."

Kurt frowned at Michelle. Her words were honest and real. Kurt tried to silence the damned voices that were screaming in his head. Kurt didn't want to hurt Michelle, she was his friend, and at this very moment, she was afraid of him.

"We know what you are thinking. Don't you dare try to subdue us, you little shit! We are in control right now, and we know what's best for you."

Taking a deep breath, Kurt closed his eyes and thought of the one thing that eased his mind. Kurt thought about how much he wished Leah was here with him. Kurt yearned to hear her whisper to him that everything would be ok. The fury and rage that Kurt was holding within instantly vanished. When Kurt reopened his eyes, the voices in his mind were quiet, and his eyes had returned to normal. However, Michelle kept her weapon trained on Kurt. Kurt looked at Elias, who lay on the cold ground, rubbing his bruised neck.

"I m sorry," Kurt said sheepishly.

"I know you are, son. I think it may be best that you leave," Elias said, wincing.

Kurt lifted the pastor off the ground and laid his hands on his abdomen.

"What are you doing?" Michelle yelled at Kurt.

"Relax, I am healing him, and then I am gone," Kurt said.

Elias felt a warm sensation radiate through his stomach, and like that, the pain was gone. "Thank you."

Kurt nodded and turned and made his way through the frightened group that stood before him. Sister Mary Francis clutched her hands in front of her chest and smiled at Kurt with tears in her eyes.

Kurt smiled back at the elderly sister and made his way out of New Beginnings Church, not brave enough to look back.

CHAPTER

39

The Master watched the spectacle from his upstairs bedroom in the New Beginnings Church living quarters. The Master saw the boy tap into his evil half. Tears of antipathy and anarchy had streamed down the boy's face freely. The Master was resentful of the boy's youth and strength. Soon The Master thought, I will again have that power and youth. The Master saw the boy hurl the pitiful has been priest like a piece of shit-stained toilet paper into the wind. Even though he needed the fallen priest to complete his task, he hated Elias Manningham and his self-righteous attitude. The thing that surprised The Master the most was Michelle. She had dared to pull a gun on the man that had allowed her to live again. And those two ancient old bats who called themselves sisters. How dare they side with the girl over the boy? It was apparent that they did not recognize greatness when they saw it. The Master forced himself to relax; his heart could barely take any more stress. This place will soon cease to exist after I regain my power, The Master thought to himself. The Master was somewhat disappointed when he saw the boy leave. However, with him gone, no one could stop him. The Master looked in the mirror and checked his tan makeup, smirking. He rubbed his hand over his wrinkled, bald head. A knock on the door startled him; The Master quickly grabbed the greying wig he had been wearing and placed it on his head without a moment to spare. The door opened, and one of the kitchen volunteers poked her head into the room.

"Sister Ana Marie, we could use your help if you're finished praying," the volunteer said. "It's been a crazy morning here."

"Si," The Master replied with a nefarious smile.

Kurt wandered around the city of Richmond for a few hours. How could he have been so dumb, letting his emotions get the best of him? Feeling dejected, Kurt wandered into an empty field that had been transformed into an urban playground. Kurt watched the young children running around in the winter air without a care in the world. They were oblivious to all the agony, sadness, and desolation around them. The ironic thing was that Kurt was as naive as they were until a few weeks ago. Since that horrible night in the alley behind Dawn's, Kurt had met demons, released a demonic entity that had been lying dormant in him, and healed those in pain. Kurt shook his head in disbelief at the events that had recently taken place in his life.

"No better day than today to ponder one's purpose," a voice said distinctly.

Kurt abruptly turned to his left. Sitting on the bench beside him, which had been vacant moments ago, was the old porcelain-skinned man from the bus in the black tailored suit.

"Are you The Master?" Kurt asked. "Are you here to kill me?"

The liver-spotted man smiled. His porcelain skin was extremely tight around the eyes as if he recently had some cosmetic work done. Removing his black fedora hat, the man pulled a handkerchief from his suit and mopped his moist-less brow. The man returned the cloth to his pocket and placed the fedora back on his head, covering his whispering white hair. "We are all masters of something, are we not, Kurt? You should not fear death. It's the ultimate release."

"How do you know my name?"

"A young man with your talents, I would be a fool not to know your name. But one question at a time, it's not like you have any place to go."

Kurt instantly felt his cheeks blush in embarrassment.

"Do not be embarrassed. We all lose control at times. You will learn from this mistake. There is no doubt in my mind."

"It's not me you should be worrying about," Kurt growled, grabbing the old man by his arm. "How long have you been following me?" Kurt asked angrily.

"Young man, it would be wise for you to let go of my arm. You are going to ruin a five thousand dollar suit."

The mysterious old stranger's sarcasm set loose a range of emotions through Kurt. Anger, fury, embarrassment, and even envy filled him. Kurt tightened his grip on the stranger's arm. If he had been paying attention, Kurt would have noticed the energy radiating from the solid muscle underneath the tailored suit. The old-timer grabbed Kurt's wrist with his free hand and looked deep into Kurt's eyes.

"Like a spoiled child, you must learn how to control yourself. You cannot get what you want all the time. Yes, this will hurt, but you have brought this on yourself."

Where the strange man's hand touched Kurt's flesh, there was a sudden immense pain that immersed Kurt's entire body. Kurt felt as if though he had been dropped in ice-cold water, electrocuted, and then stung by a swarm of bees. Instinctively Kurt wrenched his hand from the old man and stared at him in disbelief. The stranger smiled innocently at him.

"What the hell was that?" Kurt said once he was able to speak.

"That my friend was the touch of true power. Something you will never know anything about."

Kurt flexed his hand, still feeling the aftershock of the pain in his extremities.

"Let's take a walk, young man. Get the blood pumping, and I will answer any questions you have." The elderly man said, extending a helpful hand to Kurt.

Kurt glanced at the old man's hand. "No, thanks. I do not need a hand from you." Kurt said, getting up from the bench timidly.

"What is it?" the old man asked.

"Never touch me again," Kurt replied.

"That my angry young friend depends on you," the senior citizen said as he turned away from Kurt and headed casually down the street.

CHAPTER

T he incident that had transpired earlier in the day with Pastor Elias and Kurt was on everyone's mind. Michelle tried to pretend that she was fine, but deep down, she was an emotional wreck. She had to shoot a man whom she thought was her friend. Suppose if it wasn't for Kurt, who knew what would have happened to her. Trying to keep her mind engaged, Michelle helped the sisters prepare for lunch. The two elderly sisters had been quiet since the fight in the garden. Michelle thought she saw Sister Mary Katherine crying when Kurt walked away. Michelle felt sadness for the old sister even though she too felt like crying.

While everyone else attempted to prepare for lunch service, Elias had excused himself to his room. He wasn't hurt physically, Kurt had made sure of that by healing him before he left, but emotionally he was a beaten man. Elias had cast out another young man who had needed his guidance. Today was not the first time he had cast out a church member who needed his help. The memory of his prior transgression haunted him daily.

Before creating New Beginnings Church, Elias Manningham was

a respected priest in the Catholic Church. Sister's Mary Katherine and Mary Francis were his two assigned charges, and together the three of them were a force to be reckoned with. Father Elias Manningham had a reputation of being a stickler to the rules, who listened and wisely gave his view to those who requested it. He was available to his parishioners twenty-four hours a day, seven days a week.

One day Father Manningham received a visit from one of his congregation members, a young man named Jason. Father Manningham had seen Jason grow from an awkward child into that of a sound young man. Jason and his mother Ruth had never missed a service in the ten years Father Manningham had been their church leader. Jason was now a freshman in college, and he had Father Manningham to thank for that. Father Manningham had written Jason a heartfelt letter of recommendation that swayed the admissions board to let in Jason, whose past was not the greatest. Like most children in small towns, there wasn't much to do, and in Pittsburgh, Pennsylvania, there was even less. Jason had racked up a lengthy list of vandalism and petty theft charges in his short time in the world. If not for Father Manningham's letter, Jason would've fallen into the small-town way of life. He would have either been in jail or working at one of the local steel factories. One weekend while Jason was home from college visiting his mother, he stopped by to see Father Manningham.

Father Manningham hardly recognized Jason. He looked the same, but his level of confidence and self-esteem was on another level. The shy trouble maker who once slouched and whispered now stood tall with his shoulders back and spoke loudly. Father Manningham asked Jason what had transformed Jason into this new person. Jason explained to Father Manningham that he was in love. Jason went on to paint a picture of a cosmic love that transcended time and space itself. For the first time in his life, Jason said he was happy. The stars and the moon were all within his grasp, and Jason couldn't wait to experience all life had to offer.

Father Manningham sat back and listened to Jason explain how he was a changed man. However, he was terrified of his mother finding out. Father Manningham leaned forward in his chair and looked at Jason quizzically. Jason explained that the person he was in love with was another man. Jason wanted Father Manningham to come with him to his mother's home and explain to her that everything would be okay.

For a split second, Father Manningham almost agreed to go with Jason. The young man was in love, and it had changed him for the better, but the rules were the rules. The word was straightforward and not meant to be paraphrased. Father Manningham wanted nothing but for Jason to be happy, but he could not go against the word. Father Manningham agonizingly told Jason that this was an experimental phase that he was going through and that he was not in love. Going against his heart, Father Manningham told Jason if he did not stop this matter, he would be punished for eternity for his sin.

Jason began to sob. He had been sure that Father Manningham would've supported him. Jason told Father Manningham that people couldn't switch love off and on. Jason stared at Father Manningham in disbelief with tear-soaked eyes, smiled, turned, and left. That night Jason took his own life. There was a letter addressed to Father Manningham left at the scene. In the letter, Jason forgave Father Manningham for his ignorance and hoped that he would learn that the word may be steadfast, but the translation was open for interpretation. In his final testimonial, Jason told his mother that he loved her but knew that his love life would make her ashamed, and he would rather die than disappoint her.

By month's end, Jason's domineering mom Ruth, filed a wrongful death lawsuit against Father Manningham and the Catholic Church. Not wanting another scandal, the church settled out of court for an undisclosed amount and transferred Father Manningham and his two charges to another state. But Father Manningham was not the same man he had been before Jason. Now he questioned the word. His belief had caused a young man to take his life. Father Manningham found solace at the bottom of a whiskey bottle. Before long, he was unable to lead sermons or offer guidance. The Catholic Church gave Father Manningham the option to retire or go through rehab, but he refused both options. It wasn't long before the Catholic Church expelled him. Sisters Mary Francis and Mary Katherine had multiple relocation options, but out of loyalty and concern for their friend, they decided to retire to go with Father Manningham.

Elias Manningham sat behind his oak desk with the memory of how he treated Jason and Kurt fresh in his mind. Elias unlocked the bottom drawer and took out a three-year-old bottle of scotch. Elias's faith had been tested, and he failed. "Please forgive me," he said aloud as he poured himself a glass of scotch.

Through all of the chatter of the fight that had taken place earlier that day, and since those involved were currently dealing with their own inner turmoil. No one noticed the behemoth of a man wearing a jacket four sizes too large even for him, entering the soup kitchen, and taking a seat in the far corner—no one except Sister Ana Marie. The disguised nun silently acknowledged Moloch, who in return nodded to his Master.

CHAPTER

"**Y**ou understand that I cannot offer you any help. However, I may be able to fill in some of the blanks for you." The old stranger told Kurt as they strolled down the cold sidewalk. "Let's start with the basics. My name is Azrael. I am the angel of death. It is a pleasure to make your acquaintance."

"So you're the Grim Reaper?" Kurt asked, stopping in his tracks.

"No, I am the angel of death, as I just stated."

"I meant no disrespect," Kurt said quickly. "Where is your black robe and scythe?"

"You have a problem with listening, don't you? Don't you think it would be weird for me to walk down the street wearing an oversized robe carrying a six-foot scythe? Besides, I just told you that I am not death. I am the angel of death. I escort souls to their final destination."

"Okay, sure you do."

"Besides, I like my tailored suits; they make me look more debonair."

"Still, if you were the dude with the scythe, it would make you look more intimidating."

"Intimidation does not equal respect."

"Respect, arent you just a delivery guy?

"I have a vital responsibility, something you wouldn't understand. Do I have to inflict pain for you to respect my power?

"No sir," Kurt replied, instantly shutting up.

"Good. Where was I?"

"You were going to fill in some of the blanks for me."

"Ah, yes, let us continue our conversation."

Kurt and Azrael continued to walk, which led them deeper into the city. They had made it six blocks before Azrael spoke again.

"There are unusual things in motion right now, and your choices will send ripples throughout this world and the hereafter. Right now, there is a being who wishes to unlock the power of an ancient evil book. It would be best if you stopped him from doing so. Someone has interrupted the flow of things, taking souls before their time. Your friends are an unfortunate example of that." Azrael stopped walking and took an old leather-bound book with countless faded pages from his jacket. The angel of death flipped through several pages and then stopped once he had found what he was looking for. "Your friend Leah was not to be taken for another seventy years, her brother had another forty years and her mother another fifteen," Azrael read from his book. "Those souls belonged to me, and someone stole my souls. So the question is, are you going to right the wrongs, or are you going to do nothing?"

Kurt felt himself become stunned with emotions. Leah had another seventy years, and she could have spent it with him. Kurt felt his legs become rubbery, and his stomach felt like he had several bricks in it. Kurt felt himself start to wobble and would have fallen had Azrael not caught him.

"Kurt, I know this is a lot to take in. However, we don't have time for you to feel sorry for yourself. I need you to get it together."

"Seventy years? She could have been with me for seventy years," Kurt said anxiously.

"Right now, she is suffering, and you need to free her and the other souls before they are lost forever."

"Tell me everything you know about this Master," Kurt said, his eyes growing black with anger. "Especially the part about how I can kill him."

CHAPTER

43

L unch service went off without a hitch. People came, people ate, and people left. For some reason, there was an influx of new faces. New Beginnings Church served more food today than it had ever done before. It was so busy that no one noticed the large man with the large jacket get up and let himself through the kitchen and down to the storage cellar that Kurt had called home. Moloch took the whimpering Sebastian from under his coat and gingerly placed him onto Kurt's bed. The cot bowed at the weight from Sebastian. The large man and his pet would wait there until their master told them it was ok to come out.

CHAPTER 44

"The Master is the original author of the Codex Gigas, and it did take a lifetime to create. The Master traded his soul and youth to escape execution. The Devil, being the king of lies, agreed to accept The Master's soul in exchange for completing the Codex, but the Devil did not tell The Master that he would age but never die without his soul. Your soul is your life force. Without it, your body is just a shell," Azrael explained to a confused Kurt. "Let's say the Master is a 1975 mustang and his soul was the engine. If we remove the engine, the mustang is merely a shell. The Master exists through spells and witchcraft, leaching years from the souls he's stolen. The Master remembers that the Codex Gigas contains restorative soul incantations. The Master began searching for the Codex Gigas, but it was lost for centuries. The Master devises a plan to steal the Codex on its worldwide tour and rejoin his soul to his aging body. From my calculations, there are over three thousand souls trapped inside of Sebastian. Souls that are rightfully mine to guide to their final resting place. Once the souls are exchanged and an incantation read, The Master would get his soul back in return. With another spell from the

Codex and sacrificing those who nourish the less fortunate yet seek no reward, The Master could reverse his age and become immortal."

"Why don't you guys just stop him?"

"By you guys, I assume you mean us angels? We are forbidden from interfering directly in human events. We are only allowed to watch from the sidelines. We offer words of encouragement, let people know we love them and are here for them."

"So isn't this interfering? Telling me all of this?" Kurt asked skeptically, his mind racing from all the information he was trying to process.

"No, considering that you aren't technically human, but that is another story in its self, I am not breaking any rules by talking to you. And you don't abide by any of our rules."

"What's that supposed to mean? I'm a good guy," Kurt responded angrily.

"Are you? Think of all of the things you have done in the last few days. Allow me to explain specifically. You hurt those three guards at that drug house. That was hard to watch in itself, but that was nothing compared to what you did at Club Oblivion. You unleashed pure hell on earth on those poor individuals. You've let anger cloud your judgment. So no, you do not abide by the rules," Azrael said. "You are no better than those you seek to destroy. Yes, you've done some good, that I cannot deny. We must hold someone with your abilities to a higher standard. It is an angel's responsibility to serve and assist. Those are the rules handed down to us. Nowhere does it say we are to destroy and injure mortals."

"I don't know what I am, but I'm positive I'm no angel. Therefore your rules mean nothing to me. Besides, some rules were made to be broken. Those people in Oblivion were given a choice to leave. It's not my fault they were too stupid to want to live. My friends weren't given a choice of whether to live or die. They were just killed and ripped from my life. So, yeah, I may have overreacted in some instances, but for a guy who's trying to make sense of things, I think I've done a pretty stand-up job. My friends are dead and are inside some obese hell dog, and you are asking for my help, so before you judge me, look at yourself. Just tell me how to free my friends and destroy The Master."

"You must slay the Ravisher, Sebastian as you know him. This task will not be easy since the beast has armored skin, but there is one weakness. There is a soft spot approximately dead center on his stomach. You will be able to figure it out once you see it."

"How do I find The Master?"

"To complete the trade of souls, The Master must find someone who like himself has lost their faith and questions their purpose. For example, let's say a former respected priest recently opened a church here in this city to feed the homeless. Let's say this former priest wonders how he will keep his church's doors open every day. Let's say this former priest has begun to question if he is even making a difference. That person would be a prime candidate for The Master."

"The Master is going after Elias Manningham at New Beginnings Church?"

"He is already there. He has been there the entire time disguised as Sister Ana Marie."

CHAPTER

"Sister Anna Marie, the old Peruvian nun? Shut up!" Kurt retorted. "Do you think this is some joke?"

"I am not joking. Now please lower your voice," Azrael said calmly, his grey eyes blazing.

"Don't tell me what to do. You haven't done anything but cause me grief. You want me to believe that a sun-dried-up old nun is The Master. Why should I believe you?"

"I have no reason to lie. I want my souls. I don't want hell to have them. So you stop The Master, free the souls and wa-la, job well done. I know it's hard to believe that Sister Anna Marie is The Master, but it is the truth. Step away from the situation and think. Think hard from the beginning. You knew something was off about her."

Kurt closed his eyes and tried to clear his mind. Azrael was right; there was something off about the old nun. Sister Anna Marie lied about speaking English, but that wasn't enough to claim that she was The Master. She was extremely quiet, but that too wasn't enough evidence. Sister Anna Marie was excited to see the Codex Gigas, but so was the rest of the city. Kurt closed his eyes even tighter, trying to recall every moment with the sun-drenched nun. The first time he had encountered her, she seemed nervous, laughing like she understood all the jokes pretending to fit in. Then it hit Kurt; the first time he had met the nuns, he instantly noticed how vibrant and colorful Sister Mary Francis and Mary Katherine's eyes were. Sister Anna Marie's eyes were completely black.

"Her eyes, they are like mine when I lose control. Her eyes were black. Subconsciously I noticed it, but I forgot," Kurt said, opening his eyes.

"You forgot because The Master wanted you to forget. The Master hasn't survived all these centuries by luck. Witchcraft and devil magic is powerful and can confuse us all. You know they say the eyes are the windows to the soul," Azrael said aloud as he patted Kurt on his back. "You should keep that in mind the next time you decide to lose control and listen to those asshole voices in your head."

CHAPTER

46

Michelle had just finished doing the lunch dishes when she thought she heard a sound coming from downstairs from Kurt's room. At first, Michelle paid no attention to the noise. Every time there was a breeze, Michelle thought the old building would collapse. Michelle knew the building creaked and moaned all of the time. Michelle dismissed the noise until she heard what sounded like an animal growling coming from the storage room. Michelle walked to the door and peered down the dark stairwell.

Moloch was getting restless, as was Sebastian. The storage room that reeked of the boy was small and dark. Even though both Moloch and Sebastian could see in the dark, the room appeared to have extra shadows. Both Moloch and Sebastian were becoming more and more restless and were ready for battle. Sebastian growled, his way of telling Moloch that he was anxious. Moloch held one of his large fingers to his lips, telling Sebastian to be quiet. However, it was too late. Someone from upstairs called down.

"Kurt, are you down there?" Michelle called out, her voice echoing back to her.

Michelle strained to listen. It was quiet, too quiet. Like someone was trying to remain unnoticed. Maybe Kurt had come back without anyone noticing? Not liking how things went earlier that day, Michelle decided to go downstairs and apologize to Kurt.

Moloch heard footsteps on the stairs descending one at a time. As quickly as he could, Moloch tried to hide, but there was nothing for a man his size to hide behind. Sebastian and Moloch were the largest objects in the storage room.

Michelle heard someone moving around as she descended the stairs.

"It's okay, Kurt, it's only me."

Michelle made it to the bottom of the stairs, only to find the room completely dark. Michelle maneuvered through the small room, trying to make her way to the light switch that hung from the ceiling in the middle of the room. From the right side of the room came a low growl. Michelle stopped in her tracks; the hair on the back of her neck began to stand. Swallowing hard, Michelle reached up and grabbed for the light and turned it on.

Sitting on Kurt's bed was the largest animal Michelle had ever seen. The dog-like creature glared at Michelle with hazy dead eyes. Drool dripped from its mouth and collected on the donated blanket covering Kurt's bed, which now bowed underneath the creature's weight. The beast growled, showing a row of razor-sharp teeth. Very slowly, Michelle began to back her way to the stairs.

"Good dog," Michelle said, trying to conceal the fear that radiated out of her every pore. As Michelle kept her gaze locked on the creature that was on Kurt's bed, she somehow missed the large man who had come up behind her.

"He no hurt you," Moloch said, attempting to grab Michelle.

Michelle let out a scream and twisted away from Moloch's grasp. She was able to maneuver around Moloch and sprint up the stairs. As she looked over her shoulder to make sure she was not being followed, something hard slammed into her skull. Michelle saw a blinding white flash of light before her body crumbled, and she fell down the stairs. Michelle's head connected with the last stair with a vicious crack, rendering her unconscious.

From the bed, Sebastian began to whimper in excitement as The Master cautiously descended the stairs.

"Stupid girl, what a waste," The Master said. "Moloch, tie her up and gag her so she cannot scream when she wakes. And while you're at it, give her some of this."

The Master tossed a used syringe to Moloch that he had acquired from one of the many addicts who frequented the soup kitchen. Moloch caught the syringe. The needle disappeared into the monster's hand.

"I can see the newspapers now. Strung out junkie kills priest and volunteers at a local soup kitchen," The Master said, watching as Moloch pushed the syringe into Michelle's arm.

CHAPTER

"**W**hy didn't I figure it out?" Kurt said in disbelief. "Hiding in plain sight, everything makes sense now. Her dark tan skin was make-up. Her Peruvian dialect or whatever it was didn't make sense. All along, The Master has been one step ahead of me because he heard everything first hand. But why did he attack Leah and me in the first place?"

"The Master is old; he knows how to fit in. Centuries of changing his appearance have made him a master of disguise. He had even managed to stay hidden from us angels, until now, that is," Azrael said before he continued. "As far as him attacking you and Leah, it is probably a coincidence. Let's concentrate on how to destroy him and return those souls to me. Those souls are mine to deliver."

Kurt noticed that Azrael was awfully possessive for an angel of death, obviously a characteristic flaw for a guy who escorted dead souls to the other side. However, Kurt knew he was right. The Master had to be stopped.

"We must divide and conquer," Kurt said aloud.

"We? Are you Frech all of a sudden? Perhaps you haven't heard what I have been saying. Angels are forbidden to interfere with humans."

Kurt looked around before he spoke. "Ok, there's you, The Master who doesn't have a soul or, as you so elegantly put it, an engine, Moloch, Sebastian, and me, what humans are you speaking about?"

"The ones that rest inside of Sebastian. Not to mention the ones that are now in danger at New Beginnings Church," Azrael said quietly.

"So you mean, I'm on my own to solve a problem you are too afraid to handle," Kurt said.

"Mind your words, you half breed! You have no idea who you are talking to," Azrael spat out. "I am afraid of nothing on this world or in the hereafter; I am the angel of death."

"Same old cocky used car salesman tough guy act. We know what he's scared of."

"Oh, ok. You can catch an attitude with me, but the people who need your help only get words of guidance. Well, I have got some words for you. Tell me how to defeat The Master. Tell me, a non-human, how to save his friends. You can at least do that, can't you?"

Azrael thought for a moment as if he was scrolling through a million-page rule book for angels before he spoke.

"The large man called Moloch is a golem. He was created from ancient clay. Most golems cannot talk or possess free will. However, Moloch is unique. Most golems are created by writing a sacred word on a piece of paper, and then this piece of paper is inserted into the creature's mouth. Moloch is much more powerful because the page he swallowed is an original from the Codex Gigas that the Master kept, one of the pages that had been lost over the centuries. The only way to defeat the golem Moloch is to obtain the page from his stomach," Azrael explained. "Then he will return to his true clay form and can be defeated."

"How am I supposed to do that? Tell him that he is obese and persuade him to stick his fingers down his throat?" Kurt asked. "Or hand him a magazine with some skinny airbrushed chick on the cover and hopes he gets the message?"

"Perhaps this will help you," Azrael said, reaching into the breast pocket of his suit jacket, pulling out what looked like a switchblade knife, and tossed it to Kurt.

Kurt snatched the knife from the air and looked at it. The six-inch knife handle was made from ivory. There were three triangles carved along the hilt of the handle. Kurt pushed one of the triangles that looked the most worn. The blade that exploded from the handle was a foot long and curved. Kurt didn't understand how a knife of this length could have possibly existed within the handle. The blade was twice the length of the handle.

Azrael sensing Kurt's awe, spoke, "The blade has been with me during the toughest battles. I haven't used it in ages, but it should serve to empty the golem's stomach. The blade is compressed spiritually inside of the handle, and it grows based on one's faith, toss it back."

Kurt sheathed the blade and tossed it back to Azrael, who caught the ivory handle and pressed the button. The sword that shot from the handle was nearly four feet long. Azrael smiled at Kurt before returning the sheathed blade.

"Size isn't so important," Kurt muttered. "So the more I believe, the larger my blade. Man, imagine if that was true for other things. Men wouldn't have to spend so much money on erectile dysfunction pills," Kurt joked, hoping to conceal some of his nervousness.

"So, are you clear on how to defeat the golem?" Azrael asked, ignoring Kurt's joke.

"Cut the page out of his stomach. Easy enough."

"Trust me, it won't be that easy, but neither will be destroying The Master. To destroy The Master, he must first denounce the source of his power."

CHAPTER 48

It didn't take Moloch long to collect the other members from around the church. The two elderly sisters who lived upstairs had been the easiest. They were working in the garden, which looked as though it had been trampled, with their backs turned to Moloch. They didn't even know he was behind them until he slammed their heads together, knocking off both their glasses and rendering them unconscious. The few cleaning volunteers didn't stand a chance, and the ones that fought back were taken care of quickly. The graying former priest had put up a good fight, and this had surprised Moloch. The man threw drunken punches and slurred profanities like a Norwegian rummager. It made Moloch sad having to club the priest until he stopped moving. Moloch tied the priest's hands behind his back like he had done to the others and carried him into the decrepit church's central corridor.

CHAPTER

"What do you mean denounce his powers? Yeah, that will be easy. Should we have an intervention? We can all sit in a circle and tell The Master how his addiction to souls hurts everyone. Give me a break."

"The Master gave the devil his soul for his life to be spared. In return, the devil breathed a new type of life into The Master. He hasn't died, and yet his body has continued to age. If you can find a way to get him to denounce the demonic power that keeps him alive, that same power source will also destroy him regardless of his spells and incantations," Azrael explained.

"So get The Master to talk shit about the one who gave him eternal life is the only way to kill him. Are you sure I can't just cut him in half with my new sword?"

"Your blade will have hardly any effect on The Master. His powers are drawn straight from the devil himself. That blade doesn't possess that much power for you yet. The Master entered into a binding agreement with the devil, unlike the golem who swallowed a written page from the Codex Gigas. Your sword will work on that creature but not The Master. The only way to slay The Master is how I've told you. I must go now; I have already told you too much, you must finish your journey alone from here. The fate of your friend's souls and those at the church are in your hands now."

Kurt looked at Azrael, his eyes pleading the Angel of Death to stay. "What if I can't beat The Master?"

Azrael placed both of his hands on Kurt's shoulders and stared into the scared young man's eyes. "You cannot fail. Failure is not an option."

"Are you serious?" Kurt said, pulling away from Azrael's embrace.

"Is that supposed to be words of wisdom? Maybe you angels should get out of the words of wisdom business. I've read better words of encouragement in fortune cookies," Kurt said jokingly again, trying to cover up his nervousness. "What else do you have?"

Kurt turned to continue to tease Azrael, but the angel was gone.

"I can't wait until I learn that trick," Kurt muttered to himself as he prepared to make his way back to New Beginnings Church to confront The Master and save his friends.

CHAPTER

50

When Michelle came to, she immediately knew that something was wrong. Her skin felt as if there were millions of insects crawling on every surface of her body. Michelle wasn't sure what drugs were coursing through her veins, but whatever it was, it was causing her heart to beat extremely fast. A bead of sweat trickled down Michelle's cheek and landed on her knee. In her drug-induced state, Michelle thought she was going to drown. Michelle struggled to catch her breath and stay above the water that had risen above her chin. Michelle thrashed around violently, almost falling out of the chair that Moloch had tied her to. Miraculously the water subsided, and Michelle was able to catch her breath.

Michelle looked around the room and thought she was hallucinating again. Seated in the room with her were Sister Mary Katherine, Sister Mary Francis, Elias, and several volunteers from the soup kitchen. Like Michelle, everyone was bound to their chairs with duct tape arranged in a circle in the church's main banquet room. Michelle couldn't help herself, and she began to cry again. It was no time before her tears began to swallow her up like waves crashing on a beach. At each crashing wave, Michelle gasped for air, determined not to drown. A soothing voice called to her, causing her to relax.

"It will be okay, don't cry," Elias called out to his struggling goddaughter. He was amazed that he had even regained consciousness after the beating he received at the hands of that monster. His left eye was swollen shut, his nose was broken, he still had the coppery taste of blood in his mouth, and he was positive that two of his back teeth had been knocked out. He had thought the freak was going to beat him to death. He had prayed, hoping Michelle would have gotten away, but it seemed like today his prayers were going unanswered.

Elias's words were like a life vest to his goddaughter. His words gently pulled Michelle out of the hallucination tide of her tears. Michelle tried to speak but was unable to; all she could do was smile a silent thank you.

The door from the kitchen opened, and the large man entered. He carried the drooling beast in his arms, which he laid in the center of the circle of chairs. No one spoke as the large man gently placed the creature down, from both fear and awe. The razor-fur-lined creature that lay in the center of the circle raised his head and growled. The growl echoed through the church, causing the entire room to rattle. The large man placed his hand on the creature's head and grunted. Moloch retreated to the kitchen for a moment before he reappeared carrying the Codex Gigas.

"That's the Codex Gigas," Elias whispered. Even though he had never seen it, he could practically feel the hatred that radiated from the worn book's withered pages. As hard as he tried to look away, he couldn't. It was as if the book was calling out to him, demanding that he gaze upon it in all of its glory.

"Is it not the most beautiful piece of work that you've ever seen. You should consider yourself lucky that I am allowing you the opportunity to fix your eyes on the greatest piece of literature ever created," Sister Anna Marie's voice called out as she too exited from the kitchen unbeknownst to the group of prisoners.

The group turned to look at the usually sun-kissed nun but were surprised at what stood before them. The voice belonged to Sister

Anna Marie, but in her place stood an elderly pale bald man clothed in a red cloak, a large amulet swung from his extra bony neck.

"I know you have questions, and all will be answered in due time," The Master said to the confused group.

"I knew she spoke English," Sister Mary Francis said. "And she wasn't a woman. She was too ugly."

"Always the jokester. How many jokes will you be able to tell if I remove your tongue?"

"Sister, why?" One of the volunteers asked.

"From now on, you will address me by my true name, Erus. Or Master to you."

The Master made his way around the captives touching each one on the head like a morbid game of duck duck goose. Most of the prisoners pulled away in fear at the Master's touch, all except Sister Mary Francis.

"Defiant until the end, little lamb. Look where your defiance has gotten you," The Master said as he wrapped his hands around Sister Mary Francis's wrinkled neck and began to squeeze.

The group of captives watched helplessly as The Master slowly choked the life out of the aged woman. Sebastian growled in approval while Moloch smiled from across the room.

CHAPTER

Kurt wasn't sure how he was going to defeat the Master, Moloch, and Sebastian. Kurt knew regardless of how much power he possessed, he couldn't beat them all at once. Kurt would have to come up with a plan to divide and conquer. When Kurt arrived at New Beginnings Church, he immediately knew something was wrong. There was absolutely no sound coming from the old church. An eerie undead silence had settled over the entire structure. Kurt decided to investigate before entering.

Kurt's eyes darkened, and his senses went into overdrive. The Master's evil presence hung in the air like a rotten stench. Kurt quietly opened a window over the kitchen sink and silently slipped in. Dishes and pots from the day's lunch were littered all over the floor. Leftover food had been left uncovered and was beginning to smell and attract flies. Taking a deep breath, Kurt tried to focus on the foreign smells that reminded him of both the night in the alley and the museum. From the kitchen, Kurt's senses directed him to the cellar where he slept. The small room reeked of Moloch and Sebastian. In the cramped space, Kurt found a syringe and more signs of a struggle.

As he bent over to pick up the needle, Kurt overheard voices through the air duct. Leaving the syringe, Kurt made his way out of the cellar.

Kurt decided it would be wiser if he observed the situation before barging in. His discussion with Azrael had made him more cautious. The Master would be a formidable foe, and Kurt needed to gather some intel before attacking him. Regardless of The Master's physical stature, he was still extremely dangerous. Kurt exited the church through the same kitchen window and stealthily made his way to the other side of the church, using several abandoned cars in the parking lot as cover. Kurt reached the north side of the church and took position behind a window covered with a piece of plywood. As quiet as he could, Kurt pulled a corner of the wood away from the window and peered in. Through the opening, Kurt saw a glossy-eyed Michelle, Sister Mary Francis, Sister Mary Katherine, and Elias, who looked like he had gone a few rounds with a former heavyweight champion of the world. Seated in the room were also a few volunteers from the soup kitchen that Kurt assumed were there as sacrificial lambs. Just as Kurt was about to crash through the window to free his friends, Moloch entered the room carrying Sebastian. Kurt watched as Moloch placed Sebastian in the center of the circle. Kurt felt his anger begin to rise.

"Well, the gangs all here. Forget what Ass-real-old told you. Allow us the honor of tearing that beast limb from limb."

From out of the corner of his eye, Kurt saw a figure enter the room. Camouflaged by the shadows, the figure eventually stepped into the light. The Master had shed his disguise and was wearing his I'm in charge red outfit. Kurt saw the surprise on everyone's face. Kurt had to quickly duck away from the window as Moloch approached and rested against the wall, inches from Kurt's vantage point. Moloch started to grunt as he waited for the murdering to begin. It was several moments before Kurt glanced through the window again. When he did, he saw The Master making his way around the circle touching the captives on the head. The Master stopped at Sister Mary Francis and exchanged some words before wrapping his hands around the nun's scrawny neck. Kurt's eyes began to glisten, black with anger. Knowing it was now or never, Kurt used his anger as strength. Kurt punched two holes in the wall, one on each side of Moloch's head, and pulled the large man through the wall.

"And now the end begins."

CHAPTER

52

M ichelle and the others watched in horror as The Master began squeezing the life from Sister Mary Francis's body. As the old nun struggled to breathe, from across the room came a tremendous crash as the large guard vanished through the wall.

"Moloch!" The Master called out as he released the old nun from his grasp. Staring at the gaping hole in the wall, The Master smiled. There was no way this boy was a match for Moloch. Moloch would exterminate the annoying gnat that was Kurt Bryant and dine on his bones.

Moloch landed on top of Kurt like a load of bricks. Kurt managed to shove Moloch off of him without taking much damage. Kurt quickly sprang to his feet, half expecting the Master and Sebastian to crawl out of the hole in the wall, but to Kurt's surprise, they didn't. Kurt immediately turned his full attention back to Moloch, who was in the process of regaining his bearings. The large man stood up and brushed the rubble off of his clothes, leaving clumps of brick and concrete in his hair and beard. Moloch looked over at Kurt and sneered.

"You die now! No more fight!" Moloch said, smashing his fist in his open palm as he began to approach Kurt. To Moloch's surprise, Kurt didn't move. He just stood there, with one hand behind his back. When he was in range, Moloch grabbed Kurt by his neck and lifted him off the ground. As Moloch drew back his large cinderblock-sized fist, Kurt pulled out the weapon that Azrael had given him from behind his back. Kurt thrust the ivory handle into Moloch's hand, but no blade came out of the handle's hilt.

"Son of a bitch," Kurt said as Moloch's fist connected to his face.

The impact was comparable to being struck by a city bus. Kurt's head snapped back viciously as blood poured from his broken nose. Moloch reared back and hit Kurt multiple times. Each brutal strike caused Kurt to lose consciousness for a brief moment. Moloch raised an unconscious Kurt over his head and tried to snap him in half over his knee. Unlike most men, Kurt's body did not break. Moloch angrily hurled Kurt the entire length of the backyard of New Beginnings Church. Kurt awakened mid-flight, right before he crashed violently to the ground. Kurt felt blood flowing from his nose and mouth as he tried to clear the cobwebs from his pounding head. Kurt winced as he attempted to take a deep breath through his broken nose and shattered jaw. Fighting through the pain, Kurt took a deep breath and hurriedly healed his injuries.

From across the yard, still lying on the ground, Kurt watched as Moloch picked up the ivory blade and examined it. Moloch's giant hand swallowed the knife handle as he tried with all his might to snap it. Moloch angrily threw the ivory handle down and jumped up and down on it, but the handle still didn't fragment. As Kurt watched the bumbling giant try his hardest to destroy the ivory handle, he realized why the blade didn't open when he used it. Kurt had used his demonic strength to pull Moloch through the wall, and when he tried to wield the knife, his demonic abilities caused the blade to remain sheathed.

"The blade is spiritually compressed. Only those who had faith could employ the blade," Kurt heard Azrael's voice speak to him over the wind.

"Forget the blade, unsheathe us instead. You need no faith to wield us, just an undying desire to cause pain to others, including yourself.

Kurt stood up, wiping the dried blood from his mouth, and began to taunt Moloch. "Hey genius, over here!" Kurt screamed, jumping up and down.

Moloch picked up on Kurt's mocking tone, and he turned his attention away from the unbreakable knife handle. Moloch lowered his shoulder, let out a warrior like cry, and charged towards Kurt

Kurt's eyes glowed black with wicked intent as he braced himself. Moloch was faster than he looked as he rapidly closed the distance between him and Kurt. Moloch noticed that Kurt again wasn't moving as he drew closer. At the last possible moment, before Moloch barreled into him, Kurt brought his knee up and leaped, his right knee connecting with Moloch's chin, causing the big man to stumble backward and lose balance. As Moloch went down, Kurt pounced on him and unleashed a barrage of anger laced punches. Kurt's possessed powered strikes connected with ferocity and accuracy, knocking chunks of mud-like flesh from Moloch's face.

"We are impressed. We did not know that you had it in you. Allow us to assist you. Unleash us again! That is an order!"

"Shut up!" Kurt screamed, clasping both sides of his head, trying to silent the dark consciousness that overran his mind. "Stop ordering me around. I am not a child!"

While Kurt was preoccupied with his thoughts, Moloch began to stir. Through the one remaining decent eye, Moloch saw that Kurt was distracted. Moloch quickly reached up and grabbed Kurt around his neck. The brute bridged his hips and rolled so that now he straddled Kurt. Moloch used his weight and long arms to hold Kurt down and squeeze his throat until Kurt's face turned blue.

"No more evil talking from in your head. Quiet time, you die now," Moloch murmured through a lipless mouth.

"Let us see how well your magical knife works now. Oh, wait, it's all the way over there across the yard. Unleash us now or be destroyed. Your friends in the church will perish, as will your friends in the beast. Unleash us now. You cannot heal if you are dead. Death is not a lesson

you can learn anything from, especially if you're the one doing the dying."

Kurt knew he had no choice. Moloch was cutting off his airflow by sitting on him and choking him. Kurt mustered enough air out of his lungs to whisper.

"Come forth."

From nowhere, the stench of brimstone and burning flesh consumed the air. Kurt screamed in immense pain as his mind, body, and soul caught fire. Kurt watched as his skin burned away. Moloch quickly jumped off of Kurt as he erupted in blue flames. The blue flames seared the ash that had once been Kurt's skin back to his body. The scorching fire quickly subsided, and when Kurt looked down, he was astonished at what he saw. A countless layer of dense shadows encased him, all separate but unified. The shadow armor was alive and snaked around Kurt, protecting him in the middle of the slithering vortex. It was as if the darkness that haunted his dreams now covered Kurt in some manner of body armor.

Moloch yanked Kurt off the ground, punched him in his face, and instantly winced in pain. Covered in the shadow armor, Kurt felt nothing, but Moloch's hand shattered upon impact. Pieces of bone and skin fell from the giant's hand.

"We are now one. You cannot cause us any harm. We will clean the flesh from your bones. You are a creation from dust. We will return you to your original form. Your flesh will be dispersed upon the wind. Death will be your last thought," Kurt and the shadow armor said aloud in unison. The voice that came from Kurt's body was authoritative and radiated with demonic energy. Kurt liked the power flowing through his body. Something about it was very archaic and ruthless.

Moloch, not easily convinced that Kurt was unbeatable, tried to strike Kurt again, this time using a piece of steel reinforcement from the wreckage that he and Kurt had created. Kurt dodged Moloch's attack and easily took the reinforcement away. Kurt swung the steel beam hitting Moloch in the stomach. As Moloch doubled over, Kurt broke the steel beam over the golems head.

"Do not show any compassion to this monster. This creation of clay has taken so much from us, and it is better to give than receive. Give him the gift of knowing this is where he dies, and we are who destroy him."

Kurt picked up the shattered pieces of steel and continued to hit Moloch. Within moments Moloch was reduced to a muddy heap of bones and clay. In a final act of desperation, Moloch tried to tackle Kurt. Kurt easily dodged the golems attack and placed him in a rear-naked chokehold. Like a boa constrictor, Kurt wrapped his legs around Moloch, breaking the golems hips, causing Moloch to fall to the ground.

"Let's destroy him now. Tear off his head!"

"No, I need the page from his stomach.

"We want to destroy him our way, and you must obey us. Our way is the only way. The angel doesn't know what is best for you."

"I said no!" Kurt screamed, relaxing his grip on Moloch. "Go away. You are no longer needed."

"Look who wants to give orders now. A few minutes ago, you begged us to come forth, and now you look to terminate our partnership. We will leave you, for now, you have tasted great power, and your hunger has yet to be satisfied. Heed these words, we will not be dismissed so easily. Maybe next time you need us, we will not come, and we will watch you die."

"I'll remember that," Kurt said as he closed his eyes and the shadow armor evaporated. Kurt felt instant regret for unleashing the demonic armor, but he didn't have a choice. Moloch was going to kill him. Kurt looked down at the destruction the shadow armor had produced. The rear-naked choke had nearly severed Moloch's head from his body. A thin piece of flesh connected Moloch's pulverized face to his neck. Even though Moloch's hips were shattered, the large man still tried to stand. Kurt left Moloch alone for a moment and searched for the ivory knife that Azrael had bestowed upon him.

Kurt dug the handle from the rubble and pressed the triangle. This time the knife blade sprung from the hilt. Kurt's hypothesis was correct. The knife didn't function when Kurt was in demon mode.

With his knife in hand, Kurt made his way back towards Moloch. The once-powerful golem was nothing more than a broken sand sculpture. Moloch attempted to speak, but no words came from the area that was once his mouth, so he tried to plead with Kurt by using his eyes.

"Don't. You knew this moment was coming," Kurt said. "You attacked me. You brought this on yourself. So don't."

Kurt plunged the knife into the fallen golem's stomach. The large giant gasped but did not scream as Kurt pulled the knife out. The odor of rotting flesh rushed from Moloch's stomach. Through all of the stomach acid, Kurt could see decomposing limbs. Underneath half of a human foot, Kurt made out the edge of the Codex page. There was no damage to the time-worn page, even though it rested in a puddle of stomach acid. Sheathing the knife, Kurt hesitantly reached in and removed the page. Instantly once the page was removed, Moloch's body turned into sand and mud and was dispersed into the wind.

"One down two more to go," Kurt muttered, making his way back towards New Beginnings Church.

CHAPTER

53

Sebastian began wagging his tail in excitement when Kurt unleashed the evil that lived inside him. The odor of brimstone and searing flesh reminded Sebastian of the underworld. A few moments later, those wags of excitement turned to whimpers of sorrow when Moloch dissolved. The wind carried particles of Moloch throughout the air. Sebastian glanced over at The Master and growled, his hackles slowly starting to rise.

"Agreed, if you want something done correctly, it's best just to do it yourself," The Master said as he frantically began flipping through the Codex Gigas.

CHAPTER

Kurt decided it would be best if he rested a bit before heading in to destroy The Master. Kurt looked at the large folded page that he obtained from Moloch's stomach. Kurt could vaguely make out a circle made up of arrows and some indecipherable ancient script written on the page. The dark satanic power being emitted from the page made Kurt uncomfortable. Kurt's heart told him to destroy the page, but his dark inner consciousness told him to hang on to it for safekeeping. Besides, a reanimation spell could bring Leah back to Kurt. After all he had been through, he would not waste a second chance with the woman of his dreams.

CHAPTER

55

For the first time in many centuries, The Master was worried. A thin trail of sweat began to roll down his old face. Not wanting to appear frightened, The Master spoke loudly, hoping that Kurt would hear him.

"Moloch was a brute moron. I have survived for centuries, and you do not scare me, boy. I am the co-creator of the Codex Gigas. I have stared into the eyes of the devil himself. You are nothing to me."

"Then why are you sweating like a whore in church on Sunday?" Sister Mary Francis said hoarsely. Her voice strained from The Master's attack. "You know what else survived for hundreds of years? Roaches. I hope Kurt stomps your ass."

The Master was shocked; even in the face of death, the old woman was still defiant. "You, my dear, will die the worst death imaginable. You will experience pain in ways you couldn't begin to comprehend. First, I will kill the boy, and then I will start on you. How can you have such faith in a boy who is a walking contradiction? He is no better than I. The same power that flows through his body also keeps me alive. When his eyes glow black, he is tapping into the demonic energies of Hell."

"He had no choice. He didn't agree to be whatever you are," Elias said, searching for the right words. "He is confused, but he is trying his best to do the right thing, but you gave up and threw in the towel. Kurt still has a chance, and when it's all said and done, he will do the right thing."

The Master looked at his captives and smiled arrogantly. "The right thing? You are full of yourself, priest. You, yourself, are no better than me. Do you know why I ended up here at this decrepit shit hole of a church? I'm here for you. You are the last part of the puzzle. To get my soul back, I must sacrifice someone whose journey was comparable to mine. You, too, have given up, yet you still try to lead a flock of drug addicts and homeless vagabonds to a better life. The road to Hell is paved with good intentions, but you question the grand plan while trying to lead. You are a faithless conspirator just like me. We are the same. We are men who have witnessed great misdeeds and wonder why they were allowed to happen. You're all idiots, every last one of you!" The Master screamed, looking at the volunteers, his eyes coming to rest on a bald, middle-aged dark-skinned black man named Earl who worked as a volunteer and frequented the kitchen for meals.

"You, for example, the book you so love was one of the main things that kept your people enslaved for so long. Ephesians 6:5 says Slaves, obey your earthly masters with fear and trembling, with a sincere heart, as you would Christ. Colossians 3:22 and I quote says, slaves, obey your earthly masters in everything; and do it, not only when their eye is on you and to curry their favor but with sincerity of heart and reverence for the Lord. All of your ancestors were kidnapped, forced into slavery, and then made to love the slave master's religion. Irony and idiocracy all wrapped in one. Like a fool, you and your people flock to this book for guidance. The same text that you love and respect was a blueprint for your submissive continuation of life. The difference between me and all of you is that I adapted and embraced change while you all just accepted what you were told and refused to question it. So don't you dare tell me about doing the right thing. I will show you the real power of the Codex Gigas. Before I rip out your souls and sacrifice you all, I will kill the boy you have undying faith in."

"Your depiction of the word doesn't make it the truth. The beauty of the book that you so hate is that it speaks to everyone differently, and that's what unites us," Elias said passionately.

"One of us is tied to a chair, and one of us is not. Let us test your conviction, shall we," The Master mocked.

CHAPTER

56

From his resting spot, Kurt overheard the conversation between The Master and his captives. Sister Mary Francis's words seemed to energize Kurt. The elderly nun still had faith in him, as did Elias Manningham. Kurt peeked in and saw that the captives were in reasonably decent shape, all except Michelle, who had a glazed, out-of-this-world expression on her face. The Master had unmistakably given Michelle drugs to subdue her. Kurt watched as the group struggled with their bounds. Sebastian saw the captives trying to escape, yet he did not attempt to intimidate them. For the first time, the beast didn't frighten Kurt. Taking a deep breath, Kurt decided it was time to act. The Master was human after all, and pride would be his undoing.

CHAPTER

The room of captives was quiet. The only sound was the frantic turning of pages of the Codex Gigas. The Master was searching for something that would help him against Kurt. Sebastian continued to lay motionless on the floor. Suddenly from the door leading into the banquet room, there were three rapid knocks.

"Hello, Master, I'm home," Kurt called out, sticking his head into the room.

The Master immediately took cover behind Michelle, wrapping a bony arm around her neck.

"Easy chief," Kurt said, entering the room, his hands raised. "I do love what you've done to the place, though. I especially like the hole in the wall. Have you remodeled?

"Jokes won't conceal your fright, boy," The Master hissed.

"What jokes? It looks like someone yanked a huge golem through the wall. Or is that some hipster wall sunroof?" Kurt said, trying to ease the tension in the room. "Damn Michelle, you look like absolute dog crap. Have you been in the fruit punch again?"

"I gave her something to take the edge off," The Master said cynically.

"Understandable. I mean, I wouldn't want to get my ass kicked by a girl after surviving for hundreds of years. That would be embarrassing. Do you mind if I put my hands down and take a seat? Destroying golems is exhausting work."

Kurt didn't wait for an answer; he took a chair from one of the lunch tables and squeezed between Earl and Elias. The Master instinctively tightened his grip around Michelle, causing her to gag a little.

"Relax!" Kurt said forcefully. "I just want to talk. Sebastian, you look worse than Michelle but better than Moloch. Don't worry, fella, it will all be over soon.

"What do you want to talk about, boy?" The Master asked.

"You, I want to know all about you before I end your miserable existence," Kurt said, smiling.

"End me?" The Master said, insulted. "I've been around longer than you can imagine. I've...."

"Yada, yada, yada," Kurt said, interrupting The Master. "Who, what, when, where, why, and how should suffice."

It was clear that The Master was not used to being controlled. The Master's pale face grew scarlet in irritation. The Master was losing control of the situation and would momentarily lose the rest of his composure, followed by his life.

"Cats got your tongue," Kurt said, leaning his chair back balancing it on two legs like a self-assured elementary school child. "Here's what I know. You were a monk who was scheduled to be walled up alive. What the hell did you do to get walled up? I bet it was something crazy. Did you take relations with a donkey or a horse? I bet at your height it was something smaller like a chicken or something."

The Master was not amused as he again tightened his grip around Michelle's neck.

"Right, no jokes, sorry. Where was I?"

"Walled up, monk," Sister Mary Katherine called out.

"Yeah, okay, for some reason, you promised to create a book in one single night to glorify your monastery forever and include all human knowledge. At some point, you realized that you couldn't complete your task. So you pleaded to the Devil to exchange your soul for his help completing the book, and the rest they say is history."

"You are intelligent, it seems," The Master said, loosening his grip around Michelle's neck.

"Not really, just reciting the facts from the museum," Kurt said with a shrug, still balancing on his chair. "But the Devil tricked you. The Codex would take a lifetime to create, so when you were done, he took the years from you."

"You were a man of the church, and yet you chose evil over good. Regardless of what you think of me, I may have given up hope, but you chose evil. Why would you do that?" Elias asked.

"Why?" The Master hissed. "All my life up to the point of writing the Codex, I was a perfect monk. I followed all the rules, lived my life by the word. I did all I was supposed to do. But in my time of need, the word abandoned me. The other monks were jealous of my honest life. They spread lies about me. They accused me of consorting with Satan, and since I was already accused' I figured I might as well do it. Do you have any idea how it feels to be abandoned by your beliefs? To do what you were supposed to do and still be punished. My beliefs left me, and therefore left me no choice."

"There is always a choice," Elias said disappointedly.

"Is there Father? Again, we are both here today based on the choices we've made. Look at where you are and look at where I am. You're going to die, and I am about to ascend to immortality," The Master said, sneering.

"Wow, someone's a little defensive," Kurt said jokingly. "You would think after all these centuries of looking like a troll, you would have thicker skin."

"Shut up!" The Master screamed at Kurt.

Kurt could tell The Master was near the edge. All that was needed was a little push.

CHAPTER

"I hate to be the bearer of bad news, but I can't let you carry out your plan," Kurt explained, placing his chair back on all fours.

"Excuse me," The Master said, preparing to tighten his grasp on Michelle's neck again.

"Look, these orders came from Hell," Kurt said, lying, hoping The Master took the bait.

The Master shot Kurt a perplexed glance.

"Really, how did you think that I knew how to slay Moloch? What do you think happened to Cilia? I'll tell you. I ended her existence. I even know about the soft spot on the underside of old Sebastian there," Kurt explained, hoping that The Master believed the lie. He even pulled out the page he took from Moloch's stomach and waved it around like a signed contract. "It's all right here on this page."

"What?" The Master asked, worry beginning to creep into his voice.

"Yeah, you see, you willingly exchanged your soul, but now you are trying to get it back. Hell doesn't do take-backs," Kurt lied, pointing to the Codex page as if he was reading from it. "You should be grateful that you've been allowed to carry on all these years.

Kurt could see the ancient wheels turning in The Master's head. It was now or never, send him over the edge or die trying.

"Don't shoot the messenger. I'm just doing what Hell told me to do," Kurt finished, holding his hands up in mock surrender placing the Codex page back in his pocket.

"Throughout my life, I have been stabbed, shot, hung, thrown from moving cars, poisoned, and drowned, but I have never died because I have trusted Hell and its greatness."

"Well, it's apparent that you were not well-liked," Kurt said.

"I am destined to walk this world forever. Man today needs someone who can lead them, and I am that person," The Master confessed, not paying attention to Kurt's jokes. "And once I transfer the souls and sacrifice these people I am to be rewarded, I will be reborn. I will be immortal.

"If you can't trust Hell, who can you trust?" Kurt said, shrugging his shoulders.

"I knew there was a catch," The Master barked.

The excitement that was boiling in Kurt's stomach was almost too much to contain. Kurt grinned casually and prepared to go in for the final blow.

"Seriously, the Devil is the king of lies and deception. Did you think that you could buy back your youth and soul? Hell just wants the pure souls you have collected over the years. Dont tell anyone I told you, but this was the plan, you would exchange the souls you have collected, and Hell would return your soul to you. When the transaction was complete, I was to destroy you, and your soul would return to Hell to be punished for eternity. The man downstairs would get to keep the pure souls and be able to torture you just for the fun of it. I'm just trying to save you an eternity of pain."

That was it. Kurt's trap was set. If The Master didn't fall for it, Kurt would have to try something else. What it would be, he didn't know. Kurt watched as The Master went through multiple levels of emotion. Betrayal, rage, anger, and the last was defiance. Kurt could tell that The Master had fallen for the trap.

"I won't be played as a fool. I have survived all these years not because of Hell but because of me. I did all of the work. I came up with the disguises, the potions, and the healing spells. The Devil can stay down in Hell. He is beneath me and my intelligence. I won't be his servant anymore. I am done! I will get my soul, and I won't take no for an answer!" The Master screamed hysterically, his face contorted grotesquely in anguish and fear.

"Well, if that's how you feel," Kurt said. "Are you sure you don't want to rethink this?"

"There is nothing to rethink. I am finished!" The Master shouted.

"In more ways than one," Kurt mumbled under his breath.

CHAPTER

59

After the Master's hysterical outburst, everything happened simultaneously. The Codex Gigas, which had been open outside the circle of captives, slammed shut forcefully. Sebastian sensing the pressure change that was taking place in the room began to whimper loudly. The air in the room became humid and heavy and extremely hard to breathe. The Master started to sweat profusely.

"Well, that's that," Kurt said as he got up from his chair.

"Sit down!" The Master exclaimed hoarsely.

"Or what, you are going to kill Michelle? I doubt it. You just denounced your power source. I'm surprised that you are still standing. I was expecting that you would burst into flames," Kurt said as he began freeing the captives.

"I said sit down!" The Master screamed, taking a step towards Kurt.

The Master had barely taken a step before one of his ancient femur bones snapped loudly. The Master shrieked in pain. As he was falling, he extended his hands, trying to catch himself, but instead, he shattered both of his wrists on impact.

"That looks like it hurt."

"You tricked me," The Master gasped through clenched teeth, pain overtaking his face.

"Tricked, lied to, it's all the same. I never met the Devil, nor have I gotten any information from Hell. Even though you are old, soulless, and ugly, you are still human. I know that no one likes to be made to look like a fool. So it was easy," Kurt said as he continued to free the captives stepping over The Master.

Once the captives were all free, Kurt immediately went to Sister Mary Francis and healed her throat. The old woman grabbed Kurt and hugged him, her tears wetting Kurt's shirt. Kurt looked down at the old nun, kissed her on her dry old cheek, and smiled at her. The two needed no words to convey how they felt. Kurt broke the embrace and made his way to Michelle. Kurt found the injection point and placed his hand on it. Within moments Michelle was her old self, coherent and conscious. Michelle hugged Kurt and whispered the words thank you. Kurt nodded and turned his attention back towards The Master. Elias gathered up the captives and ushered them out of the room, but he stopped and placed a hand on Kurt's shoulder before he left.

"What are you going to do with him?"

"I'm going to end this," Kurt said quietly.

Elias nodded and squeezed Kurt's shoulder, and exited the room.

Kurt was surprised that the former priest didn't give him a lecture about right and wrong. Kurt walked to the door and turned the lock so that no one could disturb him. Kurt turned and looked at The Master, who had managed to sit upright beside Sebastian. The two of them reminded Kurt of a distressed greeting card. The Master had his broken arms around Sebastian's neck. The beast nuzzled the Master and licked his face.

Kurt pulled the ivory handle from his pocket and flicked the button. A ten-inch blade exploded from the handle. The Master's eyes grew wide at the sight of the blade.

"I've seen that before. Who gave you that?" The Master asked before answering his question. "Azrael. The old angel who dresses like a Capone era gangster."

"You know him?"

"He is the reason we ended up in the alley behind your friend's bar. He confronted us as we were stealing souls from the newborn ward of a hospital in D. C. In all my years, I had never seen a real angel, and then there he was. Not like I imagined at all, old like me dressed in all black. He was whining about how those souls belonged to him. Said I had no right to steal from him. He said he would find a way to stop me. Then he attacked with that weapon, and then he was gone. Sebastian picked up his scent, and we chased him. The scent led us to you, and I assume that Sebastian couldn't differentiate between you and him since your healing abilities are divine. We lost Azrael but decided to take out our anger on you and your friends. It was an accident we found you, but there were pure souls inside of that bar, so it was still a win for us."

Kurt dropped his knife and sank to the floor. It was all an accident. They had been after Azrael and not him. If Kurt had only stayed inside that night, Leah and all those from Dawn's would potentially still be alive. Kurt began to feel nauseous and lightheaded. It was Azrael's fault that his friends were gone. He now had answers to the main question. Why.

"Trust no one. Everyone has a hidden agenda, even us. There is no such thing as a good person, just the absence of bad intentions."

"What's going to happen to me?" The Master said, gasping, trying to catch his breath.

"I don't know, and I honestly don't care."

The Master looked up at Kurt and self-consciously spoke. "In the end, everyone prays regardless of what they believe. All I want is one more day after a lifetime of pain. You will experience this soon. Una manet nox et calcare solum iter mors."

"We know you can't understand what he just told you, so allow us to translate what he wasted his last breath saying. One night awaits us all, and the road to death shall only be tread once. We will not waste

our last breath being philosophical. Eat shit and die would've been a more fitting phrase to end it all."

Unlike Moloch, the Master did not turn into sand. The Master took one more deep breath into his liquefying lungs before he died. Kurt watched as The Master's body began to decompose right in front of him. The Master's skin began to darken as his flesh began to rot and fall from his limbs. Smoke started to rise from The Master's body before he burst into blue flame. The Master burned for a few minutes, and then he was gone. There was nothing left after centuries of life.

Kurt felt as if The Master's death had lifted a giant two-ton weight off of his shoulders. He had destroyed The Master, yet there was still an emptiness in his heart. Even though The Master was dead, so were Leah, Jacob, and not to mention countless others. Kurt looked down at Sebastian, who seemed to sense Kurt's sorrow. The beast stuck out his tongue and licked Kurt's boot before resting his head on it. Kurt looked down at Sebastian, who seemed to know that he was next to perish. Kurt picked up his knife, pulled out a chair, and sat down. Sebastian let out a whimper of inquiry.

"Soon, boy, I've got some loose ends to tie up," Kurt said, petting the beast behind his ears. "Azrael, I know that you can hear me. Get your ass down here!"

CHAPTER

A zrael appeared as if he had been in the room the entire time. Azrael glanced down at the primordial ooze that was once The Master with pleasure in his eyes. However, upon noticing Sebastian, the joy instantly faded.

"Why isn't he destroyed?"

"Sit down," Kurt growled, kicking a chair to Azrael.

"I don't have long. I'm busy," Azrael said, kicking the chair back at Kurt.

"Then you should probably shut up," Kurt snarled, his eyes beginning to darken, the anger in his voice reverberating off of the walls of the dusty old church.

"There you go, don't take any of this angels bullshit."

"You attacked The Master and his cohorts at some hospital. Once you realized that The Master was technically human, you fled because you aren't supposed to interfere with humans directly. You led them right to me. Knowing that your actions were the reason my friends died, you felt obligated to help me, but you would get your souls in return, and I could kill those who caused me so much pain. Now that I know the truth, we are going to negotiate."

"I do not make deals. You are in no position to speak to me like this. I am the angel of death," Azrael said, the air crackling with energy as his voice became extremely deep.

"If it's a fight he seeks, we will be happy to introduce him to agonizing pain."

"I am not afraid of you. I'm not sure what I am, but I'm pretty positive that I could hurt you, and you know it. Yes, you are the angel of death, and if you want these souls, you will listen to what I want. I'm pretty sure that it's against some code of conduct for an angel to lie," Kurt said menacingly, his eyes continuing to darken. Kurt rose from his seat, his fist clenched. Unsure of what the outcome would be if he were to engage Azrael, Kurt was prepared to call upon his newly acquired demonic shadow armor if things got too intense.

"We haven't dined on angels in eons. This angel of death isn't as powerful as other angels we've feasted upon."

Azrael looked at Kurt and nodded. Kurt was surprised. Perhaps he was more powerful than he realized.

"What can I do for you?" Azrael asked, not willing to endanger his souls.

"I wish my friends were still alive, and I wish that I had never met you or any of the other abominations I've encountered. I wish that I was normal, but something tells me I will never be normal ever again," Kurt said, taking a moment to think before he spoke again. "I want you to place some encouraging words to the police department. Elias Manningham and the sisters obtained the Codex Gigas from the thieves who stole it. Therefore making them the recipients of the museum's reward, you will find some way to double that reward. The museum curator who still sits in jail, you will have the charges dropped against him. Oh, and I want you to get lost when all this is over."

"What makes you think that I can do these things?"

"If you want these souls, you will do it or, I will keep Sebastian as a pet, soul's and all."

Azrael closed his eyes for a moment and took several deep breaths as if he were in a trance. "Done. All the things you've requested are complete."

"That was quick. Maybe I should have asked you to fix the economy or clean up the environment. How do I know these things are done?"

"Because I said they were," Azrael said, annoyed. "Now hold up your end of the bargain."

"No problem," Kurt replied, pulling the ivory knife from his pocket, making his way towards Sebastian. "It's time, boy."

Kurt expected Sebastian to put up a fight, but he didn't. Sebastian rolled onto his back, his paws raised as if he wanted his stomach scratched. Kurt unsheathed the ivory handle's blade and bent down. Kurt saw the weak spot that resembled a small transparent circle and placed his hand over it. Sebastian let out a whimper and licked Kurt's hand in what was assumed to be an apology.

"One more thing," Kurt said, looking at Azreal.

"No, give me my souls now!" Azreal said, his eyes fixated on Sebastian.

"It's like he needs a fix or something. Possession is nine-tenths of the law, you know, or at least that's what we've heard. You could rightfully keep these souls if you wanted."

"Sebastian doesn't die. He was just doing what The Master told him. He's innocent in all this."

"Innocent? This beast swallowed thousands of souls that rightfully belonged to me," Azreal began until he heard how he sounded. "This creature killed your friends and ruined your life, and you wish for him to live."

"Some of us are products of our environment, but it doesn't mean we don't deserve second chances."

"What if I say no?"

"Then me, Sebastian, and these souls get to know each other. Maybe we'll take road trips and see the world, play fetch in the park, or just go on long walks after dinner."

"Alright!" Azreal interrupted angrily. "Just give me back my souls!"

"Angel with an addiction. That's another sweet band name."

Kurt timidly looked at the ivory handle in his hand, but he couldn't bring himself to hurt Sebastian for some reason. The Master, Celia, and Moloch were all disposed of, and now Sebastian was alone like Kurt. Frustrated by Kurt's indecisiveness, Azreal shoved Kurt to the side, pulled an older ivory curved blade from his back pocket, and plunged it into Sebastian's stomach. Sebastian yelped in pain and passed out, his tongue hanging from the side of his mouth. From the transparent circle on Sebastian's stomach, an opaque mist emerged. Kurt knelt by Sebastian to check to see if he was still breathing. The unconscious beast was breathing and deflating at the same time. Kurt turned to watch Azreal reclaim his lost souls but was appalled at what he saw. The old angel dressed in his three-piece suit had managed to unhinge his jaw, so now his mouth hung down to the middle of his chest. The mist circled the old pale angel of death before entering his mouth. Kurt found it somewhat disturbing that Azrael collected souls similar to the way that Sebastian had. Azrael gathered up the souls within mere minutes. Sebastian, who was once the size of a small car, was now a tiny puppy's size. The once ferocious beast woke up, stretched, and looked up at Kurt, his tail wagging frantically. Kurt picked Sebastian up and wrapped him in his sweatshirt.

"Kurt," Azrael called out. "I have one last thing for you. Let's call it a gesture of my appreciation."

Azrael opened his mouth, and from the mist that he had just consumed, Leah emerged, her body translucent and floating in the air. Kurt placed Sebastian back on the ground and ran to Leah. Kurt tried to wrap his arms around her only to find he could not hold her. His arms went right through her. Not willing to give up that quickly Kurt again tried to hold Leah and the result was the same. Kurt longed to feel Leah's tender touch.

"I knew you would come for me. Even when I was in the darkness, I knew you would find a way to free me. Listen to me, Kurt. I will always love you regardless of what you do. I may not be here with you physically, but our love knows no distance. I will guide you from afar." Leah said as she leaned in and whispered into Kurt's ear. "I will love you from now until eternity. If you feel as if you cannot go on, remember my love and let it guide you."

"If you only knew what I've become since you've been gone. You wouldn't say that."

"It wouldn't change a thing. Even if your heart becomes as dark as the demons that reside in your mind, I will still love you. I will reside in the shadowy part of your heart if I have to. If you live in the darkness, then I will too. Nothing grows where it is dark, but our love will find a way," Leah said, kissing Kurt with her ghostly lips. "When you feel like giving up, and you don't think you can go on, think of me."

With those parting words, Leah disappeared along with Azreal. Kurt bent down and picked up Sebastian

"Guess it's you and me now, boy."

"And us, we will always be here for you."

CHAPTER

Richmond Free Press - Codex Found:

Authorities say a spiritual advisor has recovered the priceless artifact known as the Codex Gigas. Elias Manningham and two of his followers from the New Beginnings Church were able to obtain the invaluable book from two suspects, who remain at large. The suspects are wanted in connection with the murder of several security guards at the Virginia Museum of Fine Arts. The suspects are described as two white males with brown hair standing approximately five feet ten inches, wearing blue jeans and grey sweaters. All charges against Harold Wells, the museum curator, have been dropped.

According to a spokesman for New Beginnings Church, the two suspects who stole the treasured Codex Gigas believed the book was cursed and wanted to dispose of it. Museum officials state that the Codex Gigas has not been damaged in any way. The priceless work's reward has doubled thanks to an anonymous donor and will go to Elias Manningham and his congregation at New Beginnings Church. When asked what the former priest would do with the money, one of the elderly women who accompanied him answered with, "Help heal this city and fix this dump up."

Richmond Free Press: Three men released from the hospital.

Several men who were hurt in an assault in a known drug house a few weeks ago will be released from the hospital today. Adam Taylor, Manny Perez, and Jahiem Jones were injured by what police think was a drug deal gone bad. Adam Taylor was paralyzed in the attack. Manny Perez lost the use of his right hand, and Jahiem Jones suffered brutal facial lacerations in the altercation. A fundraiser will be held today at Monroe Park for the three men to pay for physical therapy and modifications that have to be made to Adam Taylor's mother's home since it is not wheelchair assessable.

CHAPTER

I t had been six days since Kurt had defeated The Master. Now that The Master was gone, Kurt wasn't sure what he was supposed to do next. Kurt and Sebastian were in the kitchen of New Beginnings Church eating an apple and reading the newspaper when Elias, the two elderly sisters, and Michelle entered the kitchen. Things had been quiet at New Beginnings Church for the past couple of days. Miraculously none of the volunteers present during The Master's attempt to obtain their souls remembered anything. The only ones who remembered were the five that were currently in the kitchen. The last thing the volunteers remembered was the fight between Kurt and Pastor Manningham. Kurt assumed this was part of Azrael's cleanup plan. To keep their secret safe, the group agreed never to talk about what happened in front of anyone besides themselves. Assuming that he was in the way, Kurt got up from the table and gathered his newspaper when Sister Mary Francis spoke.

"Just because you saved the day, don't think you get to leave. Someone has to make sure Sebastian is taken care of. Besides, without me, who would make sure that you two ate."

Kurt looked at the elderly sister and gave her a timid smile.

"We'd like you to stay, Kurt. We are all we have," Michelle added.

"Please, son, stay," Elias said. "We need another man around here. You could help out here in the kitchen, that is, if you want to. I will remodel this dump with the reward money, as Sister Mary Francis so eloquently put it. We're also going to buy some more property in the area and open up a community center to help this city get back on its feet. I could use your help."

Kurt thought for a moment. Over the last couple of weeks, Kurt had lost Leah, the love of his life and his best friend, but had met several new friends in Pastor Manningham, the two elderly sisters, Michelle and Sebastian. They were now his make-shift family.

"Of course I'll stay, but there is something I have to do first."

CHAPTER

63

I t didn't take Kurt long to get to Monroe Park. The park was a few miles away from New Beginnings Church. Monroe Park, in its hay day, was a popular place to take children. Once the jewel of the city, but like everything else during this unprecedented recession, Monroe park had been in decline for years. The parks department had its funding cut to nothing and couldn't maintain all the parks in the city, so the residents who lived around the park pitched in and kept it clean. It wasn't unusual to see neighborhood residents hard at work cutting hedges and picking up trash.

In the middle of the park, there were several picnic tables underneath a giant party tent. Music blared from a wireless speaker located in the center of the tables. The rest of the tables were covered with food and gift bags, which Kurt found ironic. These men being honored hurt people for a living. Now they were being showered with gifts.

About ten yards from the gift mountain, at another table, sat the three men who were the guest of honors for this party, their friends and family surrounding them. Kurt felt instant shame for what he had done to the trio. Not only had he caused them pain, but his actions had also tortured their families. Kurt was about to turn and leave when Jahiem Jones spotted him.

"What the hell? Wait a minute, cut that damn music off. That's the asshole that did this to us," Jahiem yelled.

The music came to a screeching halt. Everyone in the park turned and looked at Kurt. Several guns were drawn and pointed at Kurt, who instinctively raised his hands. Of course, he would be fine, but there were children in the park.

"Stupidity is a community issue. Shall we hold an impromptu class on small firearms? By class, we mean removing a few small arms from bodies before they fire their guns."

"Everyone relax. I am only here to fix what I caused," Kurt said, shaking his head in disbelief as he felt a gun jammed into the small of his back.

"Move it, asshole," A thick voice said from behind Kurt as he was marched in front of his three victims. "When we're done with you, you're going to wish you were never born." The gunman whispered in Kurt's ear, his voice smelling of alcohol and cigarettes.

"What the hell are you doing here?" Adam Taylor asked from his wheelchair, "Did you come to finish what you started?"

"I'm here to help you."

"Have you got an extra pair of legs with you?" Adam asked angrily. "You've ruined our lives."

"No, you ruined your own lives by dealing drugs and hurting people for a living. Next time make better decisions."

"Good idea. Insult the natives. People say we have no couth."

"You better watch your mouth," the thick voice behind Kurt said as he dug the gun deeper into Kurt's back. "Or I'm going to shut you up for good."

"Back off, man!" Kurt said, spinning around and grabbing the gun from the man with the thick voice, who was only a cornrowed teenager, to Kurt's surprise. "You should change your career path. Only two things will come if you stay on the road you're on. One you will meet me, or two you will die. Ask your friends over there about meeting me, then decide on which option you prefer."

Kurt took the small caliber gun and crushed it with his bare hands, causing the metal to split in half, his eyes turning black. The crowd drew back in fear. Kurt knew he needed to calm the crowd down fast before all hell broke loose. Kurt bounded over the table and grabbed Manny Perez, who was the closest to him.

"Listen, man, let me help you," Kurt said to him as his eyes returned to normal as he placed Manny Perez's mangled hand in his own and pictured it whole again.

The crowd watched as white energy was transferred from Kurt's hand into Manny's hand. Stunned, the once mangled hand began to heal right before their eyes. When Kurt finally let go, Manny's hand looked as if it had never been mutilated.

"What the fuck!" Someone from the crowd screamed. There were many conversations taking place about what just happened.

Manny flexed his hand in awe. He looked at Kurt and then back to his hand in shock.

"I don't know what kind of Santeria shit you are into, man," Manny said excitedly as he turned to show his healed hand to his family.

Kurt made his way to Adam Taylor and gingerly lifted the man from his wheelchair and placed his hand on his back.

"What the hell are you doing? Put me down." Adam Taylor protested.

"Relax and be quiet," Kurt murmured sternly. "You may not want to be squirming while I'm doing this."

Repairing a broken spine was more in-depth than healing a crushed hand. Kurt closed his eyes and imagined the bones in Adam's back mending themselves. Nerve cells, nerve fibers, and bone begin to heal and regrow. Within moments Adam Taylor began to move his legs gingerly.

"Steady, it's like riding a bike," Kurt said as he placed Adam down on shaky legs.

The crowd looked on in disbelief as Adam Taylor began to move his legs as he tried to steady himself from falling. After a few close falls, Adam took his first steps, and the crowd started to cheer.

Kurt turned his attention to Jahiem Jones. "I am incredibly sorry for what I did to you. You begged me for forgiveness, and I hurt you anyway. I wasn't myself. Please forgive me.

"It's cool, man," Jahiem said.

"It is?" Kurt asked, surprised.

"No, asshole, it's not. You sliced my fucking face. You think just because you heal us, that all is forgiven. What about the pain we felt before you healed us? Have you ever had to watch as your friends were hurt and you couldn't do anything to help them? It would be best if you didn't heal me. Don't put your fucking hands on me."

"Don't waste your time on this asshole. Heal him, and he's going to repay you by trying to kill you. That's what we would do; on second thought, heal him so we can kill him later. We will do more than jack o lantern his pathetic face."

"Yes, I do know how it feels to lose someone close to me. I understand the anger that almost consumed you. I know the answerless questions you asked. Why me? What did I do to deserve this? I've felt that same anger, and it blinded me. I was angry when I encountered you, and look where it's gotten you. You are angry right now, and you have every right to be. Forgiveness is the key to new beginnings. I have forgiven myself for not saving my friends. You can let me heal you or keep your scars as a reminder of what happens when we let anger guide our hearts. The choice is yours."

Jahiem glared at Kurt. "Just because I let you heal me doesn't mean I owe you anything right."

"Correct."

"Wrong, he will owe us his miserable crime-infested life."

"Then let's get it over with, and then get the hell out of here before I kick your ass."

Kurt placed his hands on both sides of Jahiem's cheeks, and the scars that occupied his face began to fade away until they were no longer there.

Jahiem put his hands on his cheeks and felt that they were normal again.

"Thanks. I'm serious if I ever see you again."

"I know you're going to kick my ass."

"That's right. Now, if you are finished, my friends and I would like to start our party."

"Enjoy yourselves. Feel free to donate some of your gifts to New Beginnings Church. Since you're all healed and have a second chance at life, gifts seem so unnecessary, but I know a lot of people who these gifts would really help," Kurt said as he turned and began making his way through the crowd that had now parted in front of him.

"What are you?" someone from the crowd called out to Kurt.

Kurt stopped in his tracks and thought for a moment.

"Who are any of us in the grand scheme of things? I'm just a guy trying to figure it all out."

EPILOGUE

"Ramon! Come quick!" Gloria Silva called to her husband.

"Gloria? What is wrong?" Ramon Silva called out, slowly maneuvering down the dim hallway into the spare bedroom that his wife Gloria and his daughter Zarah occupied.

"Shh, Ramon!" Gloria said, raising her finger to her lips. "You will wake Zarah."

"You made it sound like it was an emergency," Ramon gasped, out of breath from his nine-foot shuffle.

Gloria looked at her husband and smiled. Ramon was not the strapping eighteen-year-old man she had married ten years ago. Life had not been kind to Ramon. His six-pack abs had been replaced by a stomach that hung over his belt. The once-toned body was now flabby. The full head of hair he had ten years ago was receding, and his eyes were sunken and dull. His appearance made him look forty years older than his twenty-eight years of age. Gloria fought back a tear. She wasn't in much better shape than Ramon. Her once voluptuous body now sagged and hung on her like an oversized coat. Her once beautiful thick black hair was graying and beginning to fall out. Gloria had already lost all of her teeth. Her parents were confident that she and Ramon were drug addicts. How else could they explain their appearance? Gloria, a former beauty queen, and Ramon, a former college quarterback. To look at them these days, one would assume Ramon and Gloria were their former selves' grandparents.

"Gloria?" Ramon said, returning his wife from her internal pity. "Did you need something?"

"Yes, Ramon, look at this video. It has over nine thousand hits. I thought it was fake, but now I'm positive that it's real," she said excitedly. Gloria pressed some buttons on her desktop computer, and a cued video began to play. "The video was shot on a cell phone, but it is pretty good. Sit down. You're not going to believe this," Gloria said as she stood up and allowed Ramon to take a seat at the computer.

Ramon sat down in her vacated seat, which was unusually warm. Gloria must have lost control of her bladder again, Ramon thought to himself. The video started to play. Ramon made out what looked like a picnic or party of some sort. There was a man in a wheelchair, one with horrible facial scars, and another man who had a mangled hand. In the front of the men stood another man whose back was facing the camera. It seemed like the men were arguing when the man whose back was towards the camera grabbed the man with the grotesque hand. He held the mangled hand in his own. The man's hand began to glow white and began to heal and move.

"Wait, it gets better. Keep watching!" Gloria squealed with excitement.

The man with his back towards the camera then grabbed the other man who was in the wheelchair. The man's feet dangled awkwardly when he was lifted from his wheelchair. Then suddenly, his legs began to twitch. The healer then released him, and instead of falling to the ground, the once crippled man stood on his own. Then there was some inaudible dialogue between the healer and the man with the grotesque facial scars. After a brief encounter, the healer placed his hand on the man's cheeks, and the scars began to fade until they were gone.

"Holy shit!" Ramon exclaimed, his pulse beginning to skyrocket. "Is it real?"

"I have watched it forty times."

Ramon and Gloria exchanged excited glances; they had finally found the answer to their prayers.

"How will we get him to come here?" Ramon asked.

"We will have to find him. I was able to trace the IP address to the person who uploaded the video. He was from Richmond, Virginia. According to the video, this was three months ago at Richmond Monroe Park. Hopefully, the healer doesn't live much further away," Gloria explained to Ramon. "We can buy a bus ticket from here. We could be there in three days," Gloria continued, her eyes pleading.

Ramon thought for a moment before speaking. "If we take a bus, we will make the other passengers sick."

"It will only be for a couple of days, worst case scenario a couple of headaches, ulcers at the worst," Gloria said, trying to persuade Ramon. "This is our last chance, Ramon. If we do nothing, we will both be dead in a few weeks, then what happens to Zarah?"

Ramon glanced down and looked at his precious angel Zarah. Nine years old, the most perfect daughter in the world. The most important thing in his and Gloria's life and the most deadly. Zarah began to turn in her sleep and awoke to find her parents staring at her.

"Hi mommy, hi daddy," she murmured, outstretching her arms for a hug.

Both Ramon and Gloria gave Zarah a hesitant smile before they leaned in to embrace their daughter. Gloria's nose began to bleed, causing her to break the embrace.

"What were you guys looking at?" Zarah asked, pointing towards the computer.

"We are taking a trip," Gloria said, wiping the blood from her nose with the back of her hand.

"Yay!" Exclaimed the little girl before she frowned, looking at the floor. "What's wrong with daddy?"

Gloria turned to find Ramon on the floor having a seizure.

"Go get daddy some water!" Gloria shouted to Zarah.

The nine-year-old girl sprung from her resting place and headed for the kitchen. Once the girl left the room, Ramon's convulsions ended, and he opened his eyes, looking to his wife.

"Headaches and ulcers. Could be worse," Ramon said with a weak smile. "When do we leave?"

"As soon as we can, it will be ok, Ramon. I promise."

Made in the USA
Coppell, TX
05 November 2021

65246839R00134